GrudgePunk

by

John McNee

Cover Art by

April Guadiana

This book is a work of fiction. Any resemblance to actual events, locales, or persons living or dead is purely coincidental.

ISBN-13 978-0615752587

ISBN-10 0615752586

GrudgePunk

Published 2013 by Rooster Republic Press

www.roosterrepublicpress.com

Grudgehaven: "A city lost to the darkness, where acid rain drums on a hundred thousand corrugated iron rooftops and cold, mechanized eyeballs squint out of every filth-smeared window."

From the twisted mind of author John McNee come nine tales of brutality and betrayal from a city like no other.

A granite detective has a date with destiny at a motel made of flesh. A severed hand is on a desperate mission to ruin somebody's evening. While a mob war reaches its bloody climax, the Mayor is up to his neck in dead prostitutes.

And Clockwork Joe? He just wants to be a real boy.

Rooster Republic Press proudly presents the latest in dieselpunk-bizarro-horror-noir. This...

...is **GrudgePunk**

Contents

On a dark stretch of rain-lashed highway there's a crooked, hand-scrawled road-sign that reads:

"You are now entering the Grudge.

Only fools come clean."

In the Flesh

Clockwork Joe ordered me to take a seat, offering a cigarette from his ivory case. “I need you to find someone, Bailey.” The springs in his brass-plated jaw whined as he spoke.

I smiled as I touched a match to the cigarette. The filter tip was laced with gold. "A broad?"

Clockwork's amber and gelatine eyes flickered to Pug, the lurker in the corner, then back to me. “Yeah, as it happens. She disappeared a couple of days ago. Ran off.”

“Sure she wasn't taken?”

He nodded, grimly. “I'm sure.” The way he said this implied she'd tried it before.

“Why'd she split?”

Pug cleared his throat behind me. It sounded like sewage churning up through a drain. “You don't need to know that,” he rasped. Sounded in a bad way. I could hear him dripping on the rug.

“Does he have to be here?” I asked Clockwork.

“Yeah,” he answered.

I shrugged and shifted uncomfortably in my seat. The armchair was new – like everything else in Joe's office – and needed breaking in. What with the gold-laced cigarettes, fancy suit and new furnishings, I was beginning to form the impression that Clockwork Joe was pretty flush with cash. Hard to believe I knew him back when he was picking the pockets of bloated corpses on the banks of Fester's River. Nowadays, he was more likely the one doing the dumping. I made a mental note not to go pissing him off.

“She have a name?” I asked.

"Lena. But you can bet she won't be using it."

I chalked it on my sleeve anyways. "Got a picture?"

He shook his head. The joints in his neck squealed.

"A description?"

"Beautiful."

I laughed. I never met a dame in this sorry city could be called beautiful or anything close. But a study of Joe's face told me he was serious. "That all you can give me?"

"Green eyes... Red lips... You'll know her if you see her," he said. "Trust me. She's one of a kind."

I shook my head. "That don't help. A name I can't use and a face I can't picture... I can't go to my people with *that*. You at least have some lead on where she might have gone?"

"She never spoke of any family."

"Then I can't help you. I need more."

Joe thought for a moment, then looked over my shoulder to the corner and nodded. Pug marched up behind me and held out a steel jar. I took the jar, trailing mucus from his diseased claw, and unscrewed the top. Inside it was filled with ice and, on top, something I couldn't recognize. It was a few inches long, pale and thin. A single scale at one end, lacquered pink, the other end frayed and reddish brown.

"What is this?" I asked.

"Her finger." Joe replied.

No wonder she ran.

***

Bodies of rotting wood and metal. Polystyrene breasts fixed with copper wire. Mold and mildew between their legs to give you something to plow, rusting handles on their hips to grip as you go at it, and pipes jutting from their temples belching sulfur monoxide into your face the whole time. Those are the women of the Grudge – nothing like the creature Joe described. Grudgehaven is a city lost to the darkness, where acid rain drums on a hundred thousand corrugated iron rooftops and cold, mechanized eyeballs squint out of every filth-smeared window. I'd been pounding the streets of the Grudge longer than I care to remember and never once had I heard of a broad like that!

It took me five days to find anything. Vorozheikin ran a basement bar on the Eastside, corner of 5th and Gonorrhea. I went in for a dose of rye and came out with a lead.

“Never heard of such a doll,” Vorozheikin growled through the cigar smoke. “But this...” He raised the finger. “This reminds me of something. You ever hear of the Casa Carne Motel?”

“No,” I answered.

“A bit before your time,” he grinned. “The whole building was made out of this kind of stuff. For a time it was popular amongst a certain fetish crowd. Pleasure and pain and all that jazz. They used to say: 'Spend one night in the Carne and you'll never want to leave.'”

“Where?”

“Old Town. South of the reservoir. I doubt it's still there, but you never know...”

***

Some call it the old part of town, some call it the 'damned,' which it is, in every sense of the word. Everything south of the Gilberdyke Reservoir lives in the shadow of the Norrland Dam. There are more cracks in that thing than a Grudgehaven hooker's face and every year the old town creeps a little closer to the day the whole shebang gives way – billions of gallons of polluted water flushing it all out to sea. Those with the sense and the means to do so fled Old Town long ago, but many linger behind in its back streets and alleyways.

There were signs advertising the Casa Carne Motel along a four-mile stretch of deserted highway. I turned off and followed the signposts to the back of a mothballed casino. I almost couldn't believe it was still there – a pale, pulsating slab of pink meat standing three stories high. A blue neon light in the parking lot blinked 'vacancy.'

***

The clerk looked to be about two thirds Vaseline and burnt plastic, standing behind a tanned and calloused desk, dappled with liver spots. He greeted me with something like a smile and turned the guest book my way.

"Just the one night is it, sir?"

"Yeah," I answered, queasily. My eyes were on the wall behind him. It was lined with blue and purple veins, branching out in every direction. "I've never been here before."

"That's all right," he said. "Our rates are about average."

I took the pen from the inkwell and signed my name in the book. With my other hand I reached out to lean on the desk. It was warm and soft to the touch. I could feel the gentle throb of a pulse beneath my fingers.

I lost my cool a little, stumbled back. As I did I knocked the inkwell to the floor.

"Sorry..." I said. "Not feeling well."

"It's quite all right," the clerk replied, handing me a key. He then turned and called into the next room. "Mop and bucket needed out front!"

The maid emerged, a small woman in a PVC smock that covered most of her body. There was a scarf about her head. Her face was a clumsy collage of tin, clay and cardboard, framing a delicate pair of green eyes. She wore thick rubber gloves, but one of the fingers seemed suspiciously droopy...

***

In The Flesh

I hung my hat and coat by the door, kicked off my shoes, laid down on the bed and lit a cigarette. It was weird. The room, the motel... it was like nothing I'd ever seen. I started to ponder what I was getting myself into. The bed was flesh; soft, smooth and sweetly scented. There was a bedside table, a wardrobe, an armchair – all flesh. The walls and ceiling were flesh as well – skin rolling thick with fat in places, withered and wrinkled in others. Little tufts of hair sprouted in the corners. A light-bulb dangled at the end of a single red tendon.

I laid my head against the pillow and felt it move, slowly up and down, as though with easy breaths. I ran my fingernails along the mattress and drew blood. I smoked my cigarette down to the filter and crushed it in the bedside ashtray. The skin burned and sizzled.

After an hour I picked up the phone and called the front desk. "There's a mess in my room," I said. "Could you send up the maid, please?"

***

Minutes later she announced herself with a few light knocks. "Mr Bailey! It's the cleaner!"

I threw open the door, pulled her inside and slammed it shut behind her. She was startled, but didn't scream or put up a fight. I shoved her up against the wall, closed my hand over her face and ripped it clean off.

The flimsy mask buckled and shattered in my fist.

I found myself transfixed by her green eyes and the glistening red lips, taking in everything around between them as well – her true face of perfect, pink skin. I felt my own spit-and-sawdust heart clank a little faster at the sight of her.

It was love.

"Clockwork sent you," she said.

"You catch on fast," I replied, still drinking her in through my eyes.

The dame stuck out her chin, narrowed her eyes and started a speech that had an air of rehearsal about it. “He'll kill me. Did he make that clear? Take me back to him and I'm as good as dead.”

“I doubt even Joe would do something that crazy,” I lied. My granite knuckles traced the line of her neck. I tugged at the scarf and unleashed an abundance of silken brunette curls. They smelled of lemon.

“He doesn't own me. You've no right...”

“I'm getting paid,” I growled, breathing in the scent of her, “to do a job.”

“I can pay you,” she said, training her eyes on mine.

“You don't look like you could afford my services,” I scoffed.

She cocked her head, lowered her voice. “I can offer you something... else. Something I think you'd rather enjoy.”

She was right about that. My hands were twitching, all too eager to tear the rest of the clothing from her body. I leaned in a little closer, our faces almost touching. “I bet a go-round with you would feel like planting a kiss on the moon.”

She smiled. “Better. What's it worth?”

“I'll let you know.” I kissed her as hard as I dared, tasting her blood as it flowed into my mouth, hot and salty. I grinned. “You bruise easy.”

She spat and wiped her hand across her blood-smeared lips. “Yeah,” she said. “Like a peach.”

I threw her face-down on the bed and unbuckled my pants. “Don't worry, I'll be gentle.”

***

Afterwards I smoked a cigarette and lay counting the moles in the ceiling. The walls had blushed and glistened now with trails of sweat.

“I think I get it,” I said. “Why people come here.”

"Nobody comes here," said Lena. She was hoarse, worn out. She lay naked beside me, nursing her wounds. "Not any more. You're the only guest in the place."

"All the same," I said. "It's for pleasure. There's no pain at all. Just pure pleasure."

"For you maybe. And your kind. It's painful for me, for the motel, for flesh... it's just pain."

I took another puff, surveyed the room for the hundredth time. "Just what *is* the motel?"

She gave a little shrug. "I wish I knew."

"What are you?"

She sighed, then intoned: "I am the motel and the motel is me and all we are and forever shall be."

That didn't make a lick of sense to me but I let it slide. "So there's no one else like you, then?"

"Not beyond these walls. And I have searched."

"That how you ended up with Clockwork Joe?"

"Joe's new town money. He didn't know about the motel and I took care not to tell him."

"He's pretty sweet on you. Now I can see why."

She turned towards me, raised her voice. "Sweet on me? You think he *loves* me? He cut off my *finger!*"

I shrugged. "I've known guys to do worse things for love. And over girls who weren't nearly so... talented."

She laughed disdainfully and shook her head. "You think you're smart but you're not. Joe's not in love with me. He just wants a body like mine for himself. Before I escaped, I spent most of my days locked up in a lab with his scientists, studying my body for clues as to how they might replicate it. The finger was only the beginning. You take me back and he'll slice me wide open, putting every scrap of me under the microscope till he figures out how to make a pink skin for himself. And when he fails, which he will, he'll stitch me back together and wear me like a suit."

"That's insane."

"He's not a sane kind of guy."

I took one last drag and stubbed out the butt. "Well don't worry about it, sweetheart. I'm not taking you back to him. You're with me now. I can protect you. And anyway," I wheezed, leaning in for a kiss, "he doesn't even know we're here..."

On the back of my words came a knock at the door.

Lena shot me a horrified look. "Guess who."

***

I put my pants on and snatched up my Luger from the bedside table. "Who is it?" I called.

"It's the clerk, Mr. Bailey. Could you come to the door?" I could tell from his voice that he wasn't alone. Try as he might to sound calm, he couldn't disguise the fear.

Lena was putting her clothes back on. "Any bright ideas?" she hissed.

"I don't suppose there's another way out of this room?" I asked her. She shook her head no. "Then I guess we play it by ear," I said. "See if we can't talk our way out..."

It was a dumb move and I knew it, but it was still all we had.

"Mr. Bailey?" the clerk called again.

"Just one moment," I called back.

This time it was Pug who answered, his unmistakable growl cutting through a wall of phlegm. "Take your time, pretty-boy..."

I winced, muttered a halfhearted prayer and opened the door.

The three of them entered without invitation. The clerk first; eyes wide with panic, hands raised in front of him. Pug shuffled in close behind, pressing the point of a dagger against his back. Clockwork Joe sauntered in last, dressed in an expensive emerald green suit, riddled with holes where his joints and sharp edges had torn the fabric. There was a cold, self-satisfied smile on his metallic lips. “Hell of a place, this,” he was saying. “Can't hardly believe it... One *hell* of a place...”

I took a few steps back, moving to the foot of the bed.

“Lena!” The clerk cried when he saw her. “Lena, are you all right?”

Pug scoffed in the clerk's ear. “Look at her,” he said. “She's just dandy. You, on the other hand...” He pulled the clerk closer, raised the dagger and plunged it into his neck.

“NO!!!” Lena screamed as she tried to leap across the bed. I got in her way and pushed her back against the far wall.

The clerk, his windpipe severed, liquid ethanol gushing from the wound, sank slowly and quietly to the floor. Pug wiped the blade on his sleeve and gave me a hungry grin that said I was most likely next.

“You look surprised to see us, Bailey,” said Joe, stepping over the dying man.

“I wasn't... expecting you,” I answered.

“Clearly,” Joe chuckled. “I guess it escaped your attention that my boy Pug has been tailing you since you left my office. Five days and you didn't even smell him. Some detective...” His eyes locked with mine for a tense moment, then flashed to the girl in the corner. “Hello, Lena.”

She turned her face away.

Joe, apparently unruffled, looked back to me and lowered his voice to a whisper. “She sure is something, isn't she? You can tell me, we're all friends here. I know you had a taste. Don't try to deny it.” He drew closer still, till we were only an inch apart, his breath at my ear. “Just between us boys, y'know... I think she likes it rough. She says not, but you notice... if you hurt her just a little she makes... this kinda sound... it's like..."

Springs snapped and cogs spun. Brass and copper plating flashed in front of my eyes in a dazzling display of precise mechanical dexterity. Before I knew what had happened, I'd lost my piece.

"WHOA!!!" Joe cried theatrically, stepping back, holding up his arm to reveal my Luger proudly displayed in his closed copper fist. "Where did this come from? Bailey! Is this yours? What's with the gun, Bailey? You don't need this. We're all friends here."

I raised my hands in surrender and saw they were already shaking. My cool, calm exterior was crumbling. "Just take it easy, Joe," I croaked. "It's like you said. We're all on the same side."

"Oh relax, Bailey," Joe said. "I'm not going to hurt you. You've outdone yourself. Just look at this place! It's amazing! In fact, I'm going to pay you double. Triple! Plus bonus. And that's in spite of my very strong suspicion that you and Lena were planning to run off and leave me wanting."

"Joe, I would never..."

"It's okay," Clockwork cooed. "I forgive you. You got your head turned. I understand. You don't know her like I do. You don't know the evil bitch she is at her core. You wouldn't believe it. She's so... warm and soft and *pretty* on the outside. But on the inside... her *soul* is just as ugly as anyone else in the Grudge." He sighed sadly as he looked Lena up and down. "It was never the girl I wanted returned, Bailey. You understand? Not her heart, mind, spirit or soul. Just the packaging."

"I know," I said. "Clockwork Joe wants to be a real boy."

Joe gazed around the room in wonder. "Lordy, but do I!" He reached out to the nearest wall and ran his polished fingertips across its surface. "Beautiful," he sighed. "Can you imagine it, Bailey? How it would feel... to be forever swathed in such sensuous pleasure?"

"I hadn't given it much thought," I said.

“The boys at the lab'll have a field day,” chuckled Pug.

Joe nodded. “With the motel, yeah. In the meantime, I could get an entire summer wardrobe out of just this room. In fact...” He swapped Pug my pistol for the dagger and pressed his ear to the wall. “It's alive,” he said. “I can hear its heartbeat!”

“Joe,” said Lena, “Whatever you're thinking about doing..." She spoke with some urgency, but Clockwork cut her off.

“Shut up,” he said. “I don't need you any more, Lena. You're a waste of meat.” He raised the dagger in his fist, aiming its point at the wall of flesh before him.

“Joe, please,” cried Lena. “I'm warning you...”

Joe laughed. “*Warning* me? Pug!”

“Yeah?” the decomposing goon answered.

“Do me a favor and shoot that bitch.”

“Hey now,” I said.

Pug laughed. “Sure thing, boss," he said, then raised the pistol.

“Hey,” I said again, stepping towards him. “No! Wait! Stop!”

Stupid move. I knew I was killing any chance I had of getting out alive, of getting paid, of getting anything. I've never been the sentimental kind. But I couldn't just let them kill her.

I made a grab for the gun. Pug squealed with excitement, spraying my face with his hot brown saliva. I pushed against him and he pushed back, both of us trying to get a grip on the weapon.

Lena stood her ground, but her eyes weren't on us thugs dancing arm in arm. She was watching Clockwork Joe, screaming at him not to do it. Not to do *what*, I didn't know, but it looked like I'd find out soon.

The gun roared twice. Both bullets hit me in the gut. As sensory experiences go, I wouldn't recommend it. I rocked back on my feet, the room spinning about me. Pug grinned, ecstatic, his opponent presumably vanquished. I stared up at his face of blistering slime and saw the tension ease for just a moment. And in that moment I reached up, snatched the gun out of his hand and shot him in the head.

Then I fell. We both fell.

I heard Lena shriek and expected her to run to my side, to coo and comfort me as I bled to death. As I turned my head, however, I saw it wasn't my injuries that horrified her so. Her attention remained on Clockwork Joe, who had done nothing more drastic than stabbing a hole in the wall.

“Damn it all, Bailey,” he said, nudging Pug's corpse with his foot. “What'd you have to go and do a thing like that for?”

The dagger's blade – all eight inches – had sunk deep into the wall's flesh, so that only the handle showed above the skin. A thick smear of dark blood oozed out of the wound and trickled down to the floor.

“She's just a broad,” Joe said, though I could hardly hear him. It sounded to me like he was talking through a pipe stuffed with cotton wool. “However good she looks...” Clockwork bent over and picked up the Luger where it had fallen. “On the inside, she's just another broad...”

My ear was to the floor. I could hear something deep down, near but far away – screaming.

“...hardly worth killing over,” Joe continued, “...just packaging.”

The wall was bleeding. I could see it. The wall... the motel... the floor beneath me was weakening. Something was happening. The light flickered and dimmed. The alien screams, so far away before, were here now – in the room with us. The wall was bleeding. The wall was moving.

The wall of flesh. The skin... it ripped and rolled, coiled and churned and buckled and shivered and shook.

Joe, noticing for the first time something wasn't right, looked at me, then at Lena, then at the dagger he'd planted in the wall. “What... what's going on?” he asked.

I didn't have an answer. I was too worried about the floor bubbling up to consume us. I could feel it bulging and stretching and twitching at my back.

Joe looked about the room, reached out and took hold of the dagger. “To Hell with this spooky rodeo,” he said, pulling it out of the wound.

Pale, naked and completely bald, the body of a man slid out with it, his arms hanging down, his eyes dead and closed. The mark of Joe's dagger could be seen between his shoulder blades. Numerous other pale forms were visible just within the wall, writhing and screaming as one, their eyes aflame with fear and hatred that all fixated on Joe.

A twisted tangle of arms reached forth from the heaving mass, grabbing Joe and dragging him into the man-sized wound. Clawing hands ripped out his eyes, tore off his arms, and pounded his flimsy clockwork head into dust.

The wall was hemorrhaging badly. The thin layer of epidermis that gave the room its shape rolled back to reveal blood-soaked bodies all around us. I felt the floor disappear beneath me as I sank into the undulating mass. I pressed a hand down to push myself up, but it only sank in deeper. I felt my limbs twisted and warped, mangled indescribably.

“Lena!” I choked. “Help me!”

The girl's eyes flashed with rage and despair. Turning away from me, she nimbly hopped from body to body before disappearing through the door.

“Lena!” I called after her. “Len... Le..!”

I hadn't the breath to speak. By this point, the floor had swallowed me up to my chest. I couldn't feel my legs anymore. The heaving masses swelled all around, crushing me further still. Darkness crowded in and I blacked out.

***

Hours, maybe days, later, I... came to. I got my senses back, anyway. Some of them, that is. I couldn't say that I woke up, exactly. Not exactly.

The important thing is that I survived. If that's what you want to call it.

My wounds had healed. No pain. From what I could gather, I'd bled into the fabric of the motel and she'd bled into me. The two of us had managed to heal each other, to a degree.

I wasn't in the room any more. I was somewhere in the walls, plugging up the gap Joe had made. And already I could feel my body... changing.

I heard voices in the darkness, too quiet to make out, but as time passed and I grew more accustomed to my new surroundings, we began to develop a kind of understanding. Another month or two, I wagered, and we might be up to having an actual conversation.

This all happened some time ago. I'm part of this place now. I am the motel and the motel is me... and all that loopy bunkum.

I'm being remade from the inside out. I can feel it. I wasn't happy at first, but I'm a long way gone now. I can't wait to see how I turn out... when I'm all done.

I've had a lot of time to think since that night. Mostly I think about Lena, and the thoughts only get sweeter day by day. Even if that last ambiguous look was the only honest one she ever gave, I can't help hoping I'll see her again someday. It's doubtful. But I cling onto the memory of what she said, about this place being a part of her, and I know she'll never fit in anywhere else. I just know that she'll return.

And till she does, I'll be waiting.

I'll be here.

I'll be ready.

In the Casa Carne.

In the flesh...

A Hand Walks Into a Bar

Rhino could see his face in the bronze thigh of the girl on the next barstool.

"That's nice," he said, running his fingers across her polished surface. "Real nice."

He could become obsessive over the parts of dames he really liked, Rhino could. In the Grudge, that wasn't such a bad attitude to take – make the most out of what pleases you, ignore the rest. When the girl giggled and said, "Stop, cut it out," her breath stank like ammonia. Case in point.

Rhino straightened up and reached for his drink. "Yeah, you sure are something, all right," he said, laying it on thick. "A fella could lose it big time over a piece of strange like you."

"Oh sure," she laughed, nudging him in the leg with her knee. "I bet you say that to all the girls."

She was right, of course. He did.

Rhino drained his glass and waved it in the barman's direction. Vorozheikin ambled his way over like he was wading through soup, as if he'd rather do literally anything else than serve this pair another round.

"Same again," Rhino told him. "And whatever the lady's having."

The girl wheezed a laugh, her eyes rolling in opposite directions. Vorozheikin sucked hard on his cigar, puffed smoke in their faces and stalked away to the shelf of bottles on the wall.

Hell of a way to treat his only customers, Rhino thought.

He leaned toward her, placing his rough right hand on the clutch of greased hinges where her spine met her hips. On some girls this would be called 'the small of her back'. Not this broad, though. She just wasn't built that way.

"Say," Rhino breathed in her ear. "What'd you say your name was?"

"Agnes," she purred.

"Well Agnes," he said. "I don't think this guy really appreciates us, but I'm getting in the mood for something to eat anyway. Thought I might head over to Blinky's. They do a rib-eye special on Tuesdays that can't be beat. Maybe you'd care to accompany me?"

"Oh, I dunno," she cooed, all theatrical. "I hardly know you..."

Vorozheikin slammed a pair of glasses down on the bar, spilling liquor. "Go," he growled at her, veins visibly popping through the green scales on his neck. "Do me a favor and get out of here."

"You, uh... got a problem, pal?" Rhino asked, keeping the tone conversational.

"You're my problem!" Vorozheikin barked. "There's a card game on Ninth tonight. I could'a been closed early and halfway across town by now if not for you two."

"Oh, well, gee, pal, that's all you had to say," said Rhino, picking up his drink and turning back to the doll. "What do you say, hot-lips? Shall we mosey on out of here? Leave old Mr. Manners to it?"

Agnes' lips *did* look hot enough to scald. They had that 'acetic acid sheen' to them that all the girls on the radio spots raved about. Pouting them now, she shrugged and raised her own glass. "Oh, what the hey! You only live once."

"Thank you," Vorozheikin said, then slammed his head into the bar when he heard the door creak open, announcing the arrival of yet another customer.

Rhino grinned, tapping the rim of his glass against the broad's. "I don't recommend cards, pal," he said. "Your luck ain't so hot tonight."

"No," said Vorozheikin, straightening up and stomping away to the other end of the bar.

"No, no, no!" he cried. "Not tonight, thank you! We're clo—" He cut out mid-sentence, before he got within spitting distance of the door. Casting about nervously, his eyes scanned the full length of the room.

"What's wrong?" Rhino asked.

The barman gripped his cigar with two fingers and sucked at it, a puzzled expression settling across his face. "Nobody there," he said.

Suddenly Agnes screamed, leaping backwards out of her stool like a startled cat. She dropped her glass into Rhino's lap as she went, splashing her lime-colored cocktail all over his crotch.

"Goddamn son of a –" he began to shout, shutting up fast when he saw what she'd seen.

A hand, two stools over. It was expensively finished in varnished walnut and porcelain, Rhino could see, through the cracked knuckles of its muslin glove. Tufts of gray mulch spilled out from the wrist, where it had apparently been less-than-expertly amputated. There was a ring on the little finger – gold, embossed with a jewel of orange and red facets.

"Well now," said Rhino, leaning in for a closer look. "What do you know about th—"

He pulled back abruptly as the hand leapt across to Agnes' stool, eliciting yet another shriek from the girl.

"How the hell's it doing that?" Vorozheikin asked.

Rhino shook his head. "I don't know."

The hand drummed its fingers eagerly upon the leather seat, then pounced up again, this time landing prone atop the bar.

"Nuts to this," said Vorozheikin. "I'm gettin' the shotgun."

"No. Wait," said Rhino, inclining his head a little, just enough to get a good look at the ring. The engraving in its glazed surface read *C.M.Z.* "I know whose hand this is."

"You do?" said Agnes, her face still frozen in an expression of repulsion. It'd take her a long while to work it back into something more pleasing.

"Caligula Montenegro Zigguroth," said Rhino. The hand tapped its index finger impatiently.

The girl raised her one working eyebrow. "*The* Caligula Zigguroth?"

"Aw hell, Aggie, like there's two fellas with that name," said Vorozheikin, shooting her a withering look. Turning to Rhino then, he asked, "How d'you know Zigguroth?"

"I've done a few jobs for him," said Rhino. "Here and there."

"Oh *really*?" said Vorozheikin. "I should'a guessed the kind of work you was in, face like yours, talkin' at people the way you do..."

"Steady," Rhino growled.

"Well, since you and the legendarily wealthy old whore-master are such buddies," said Vorozheikin, "would you care to hazard a guess as to how and why his severed hand is hopping around my freakin' joint?"

Rhino had grown damned weary of Vorozheikin's lousy attitude by this point, and was close to giving him a gentle tap on the side of the head when Agnes cut in.

"I think..." she stammered, gesturing to the gesturing hand on the bar. "I think it wants to take you somewhere."

Rhino looked over. The hand cocked its thumb at him and pointed to the door.

"You could be right," he said. "Gimme some string, Vorozheikin."

"Gladly," said the barman. His hand went under the bar and returned clutching a ball of twine. "Whatever it takes to get that thing out of here."

Rhino cut a length of about six feet and tied one end to the hand's ring finger. The other end he wrapped around his own wrist.

"You're really going to leave here with that thing?" Agnes asked.

"Looks that way," said Rhino, picking the hand up off the bar and dropping it on the floor. It scuttled off like a spider across the greasy concrete, heading for the door.

"I guess Blinky's will just have to wait for another night."

She kind of smiled at him. At least he thought it looked more like an attempt at a smile, more so than any other facial expression.

"Good luck, I guess," she said.

Knowing this was as good as he was gonna get, Rhino nodded, took his hat from the hook on the wall, and fixed it firmly atop his gnarled head. Then, feeling the tug of the string at his wrist, he followed the hand of Caligula Zigguroth out the door and ventured into the night.

***

It was one of those calm evenings you rarely get in the Grudge, when the clouds roll down from the sky to coat the streets and alleyways with a thin, silvery mist. Rhino took a deep breath, feeling the sting of the fog on the back of his throat, then lit a cigarette.

The hand tugged at its leash, eager to be away. After climbing the stairs out of Vorozheikin's basement bar they turned north on 5th, veering east onto Septicemia Boulevard. Brick tenements shot up at odd angles from the cobbled streets, their walls pocked with dark masses of writhing slugs. There was nothing to do about the slugs between the rains. They just slithered out of the drains and up the sides of the buildings by the thousands, and Rhino could only marvel at how high they made it – and how quickly – before the next acid rainfall reduced their bodies to bubbling sludge and washed them all away. When dry weather returned, another million slugs would emerge to begin their march up the walls. So it went, on and on forever.

Rhino didn't mind the slugs. On nights like these, when he could walk for miles without seeing a car in the road or another person on the sidewalk, he felt like Grudgehaven *belonged* to the slugs. They had more right to it anyway.

The hand led him off of Septicemia at the junction with Sinister – crossing over into the Entertainment District.

"Just where the hell are you taking me?" Rhino asked, pausing to look back at the distance they'd covered.

The hand didn't acknowledge the question. It just kept tugging at the leash, fingernails scraping against the cement until he started walking again.

There wasn't much happening in the ED. Never was, these days. Mostly it was boarded-up bars and theaters. They passed a couple old movie houses that were still open for the late show, and the Blanko Dance Hall and Casino, where the house band was apparently still swinging up a storm. But that was about it.

From the Blanko on it was nothing but derelict buildings until they reached the bottom of Abednego Hill. The road rose dramatically here, climbing steeply toward the summit and the imposing silhouette of the Creeping Vine Chapel. Rhino eyed the road ahead wearily, observing the erratic flash of a broken streetlight through the mist. He stubbed out his cigarette and was reaching for a fresh one when he felt the tug of the hand once again, veering off into the road.

"Oh, come on, will ya?" he moaned. "I'm startin' to think you don't even know where you're –"

The hand interrupted him by slapping the asphalt, then tapped a finger on its surface and held it up. The tip was black – smeared with fresh motor oil. Rhino leaned in for a closer look and saw the wide black puddle, apparently fed by the slow, slick rivulets flowing down the hill ahead.

"Okay," he said, putting the smokes away. "All right. So you know what you're doing. So come on now and show me."

The hand answered by scuttling back onto the sidewalk and leading him uphill, following the stream of oil to the broken streetlight – and the wreck of a ruby red Continental. It had bounced up onto the curb at speed and wrapped itself around the lamppost like an overly aggressive lover. Shards of broken glass and splintered metal glittered in the street.

Rhino approached with a degree of caution, letting the hand direct him to points of interest. He half-expected to find Caligula Zigguroth behind the wheel, sliced and diced into various moving parts, but this was not to be the case. The driver, when finally he spotted him crushed into the engine block, was not known to Rhino. At least, he didn't *think* he recognized him, though it was impossible to tell, his face was so mangled. One eyeball looked as though it had been popped out of its socket on impact.

He had most likely been some kind of hood. Rhino could guess that much from the pistol holstered at his hip and the fact that his clothes were too nice for a cop. There were no other passengers in the car. In fact, there didn't seem to be anything except for a shoebox, half-wrapped in brown paper and wedged in the foot-well. The hand seemed especially anxious about drawing Rhino's attention to this, slapping its palm and snapping its fingers with incredible urgency.

"Okay, okay, take it easy," Rhino said, bending down to pick it up. Most of the paper had been torn away and the lid looked like it had been bent open from the inside. He shook it, took a look inside and was less than surprised to find it was empty.

"I, uh..." he began, dumbly. "I really don't know what to make of this."

The hand seemed to lose its patience then, scrabbling madly about the car's interior, drumming its fingers against every twisted surface until it found what it was looking for. Leaping triumphantly onto the dead hood's back, it help up a white envelope clasped between two fingers.

Rhino took the envelope and turned it over. It was addressed to THE SONS OF CALIGULA ZIGGUROTH. He tore it open and unfolded a sheet of paper on which a message had been written in letters cut out of the Grudgehaven Gazette.

IDIOTS, it read. WE HAVE YOUR FATHER. IF YOU EVER WANT TO SEE HIM ALIVE AGAIN IT'LL COST YOU FOUR MILLION. YOU WANT TO KNOW HOW SERIOUS WE ARE? OPEN THE BOX.

The rest of the letter covered detailed instructions as to when and where to make the exchange.

"So... I'm guessing you were in here?" Rhino asked, waving the box.

The hand replied with a thumbs-up.

Rhino grinned up one side of his face, looking back over at the mangled driver. "I'll bet you gave this guy one hell of a shock when you jumped out," he chuckled.

Tossing the box back into the wreck, Rhino stooped down to look his gloved companion dead in the eye, or at least where its eyes would've been, if it had any.

"You've brought me this far," he said, casting a sidelong glance at the chapel on top of the hill. "Think you can take me the rest of the way?"

Again the hand answered in the affirmative.

"Okay," Rhino said, checking his sawed-off shotgun as the hand led on. "But this had better not take all night."

***

Caligula Zigguroth's eyelids were made of soft gold. His cheekbones were platinum and his chin, which rested against his silk-shirted chest, was encrusted with jewels. He dozed now, in a drug-induced stupor, shackled to a barber's chair on the top floor of the Chemlik Makeup Company's 14th Street premises. The imposition allowed "Tollbooth" Tim the rare opportunity to get up close and personal with a man he'd only ever seen through a line of bodyguards. He made sure to milk the moment for everything it was worth.

With a mere three inches of perfumed air separating Zigguroth's polished chrome nose from his own broken one, Tim said: "Y'know, if we pounded his head into pieces, counted out the pieces and then sold the pieces, we'd probably earn enough of a fortune to make this whole ransom deal moot."

"Moot" was a word he'd learned the previous weekend. He'd been using it a lot.

"We'll do that too," said McNally. He stood in front of the dressing mirror, trying on different lipsticks. "After we get the money."

Tollbooth huffed and puffed through his nose, foot tapping well out of time to the jazz music wheezing out of the old gramophone in the corner. "I want to talk to him," he said at last.

"Do you, indeed?" McNally replied, studying the reflection of his lips and wondering what shade of mascara would pair best with "Hint of Midnight."

"I want to talk to him," Tollbooth repeated. "I'm going to wake him up." He took a quick look around, then grabbed the curling tongs hanging over the back of a nearby chair.

"Careful," said McNally. "Those're hot."

"Y'don't say," Tim muttered, stabbing the tongs into Zigguroth's thigh.

The diamond-studded pimp king jolted awake, emerald eyes popping open and mouth letting loose an almighty wail. When he screamed, Tollbooth Tim caught the glimmer of silver in the old man's teeth.

"Ah good," Tim said. "You're still alive."

Zigguroth blinked the mercury tears out of his eyes. It took a few tries, but finally the ugly red face of the hoodlum seated in front of him swam into focus.

"I ought'a say the same to you," he growled. "That, and enjoy it while it lasts." He blinked a couple more times before catching a glimpse of his wounded thigh. "You burned my suit, you son of a bitch. This was one of a kind."

"Ha! Some attitude you got! I'd a' thought you'd be more concerned about *this*," Tim said, pointing the tongs at the bandaged stump where

Zigguroth's right hand had been, only two hours previously. "But maybe it's good you're less concerned about yourself," he said, raising the tongs to his captive's face. "Seeing as how I been thinking I might cut out one of those pretty green eyes of yours. That's gotta be worth four figures easy, am I right?"

"Steady, Tee-Tee," said McNally. "Aldous wouldn't like that."

"Yeah, Tee-Tee," Zigguroth sneered. "Gotta keep your eye on the big picture. Listen to your..." He caught a glance at McNally and glowered. "You wearin' makeup?"

McNally shrugged. "It's a makeup warehouse," he said, by way of defense. "And it gets boring just waiting around here all night."

Zigguroth shook his head in disbelief. "You punks are morons. No wonder my boys bested you out of that dough."

"They didn't *best* us," Tim spat, raising the tongs again. "They *cheated* us."

"Then you're *still* morons."

"*They're* the morons!" Tim roared. "Them and you! Them 'cause they were stupid enough to think they could cheat us and get away with it, and you 'cause... well, look at you! Tied to a chair, one-handed and helpless. Every little last piece of you is worth something and what has it bought you? Where are all your armed guards now? Where's your powerful friends? Where's your freakin' muscle?"

A thud from a well-aimed boot ripped the door from its hinges and sent it crashing to the floor in a flurry of splinters. Tim and McNally both spun about to see Rhino, already through the doorway, shotgun raised to eye level.

"Sounded like my cue," he said with a grin. "Now I'm warning you. Nobody better..."

His words trailed off as his gaze fell upon McNally. "You wearing makeup, son?"

"Maybe..." he replied, trying to avoid eye contact with the comparatively un-done-up man standing before him.

"Weird..." Rhino continued. "Now what was I saying? Oh yeah. Nobody better try anything stupid."

"Wouldn't dream of it," McNally said, then went for his gun.

Rhino let rip with the shotgun, sending the clown-faced goon sprawling into a stack of old eyeliner boxes. Before Rhino could draw a bead on him, Tollbooth Tim drew his own pistol and opened fire. As he strafed past the large, stained glass window behind him, Rhino squeezed the trigger.

The blast from the second barrel sent Tim hurtling through the night in a cloud of glass shards and gun smoke. Rhino didn't see him hit the cobbles seven stories down, but he sure *heard* it well enough.

SPLAAAT.

Rhino set his gun down on a nearby dressing table, checking to see whether Tim's bullet had done any serious damage. It took him a moment to find where it had grazed his raincoat, but luckily he wasn't bleeding much.

"Rhino," Zigguroth gasped. "I can honestly say I've never been more pleased to see you."

"Yeah, it's nice to see you too, Mr. Zigguroth."

"Call me Cal. You think you can get me out of here?"

Rhino studied the chains and heavy lock keeping Zigguroth in his seat, then pulled a set of picks from his coat pocket. "Yeah, shouldn't be a problem," he said, kneeling down for a closer look. "So, uh... those friends of your sons?"

"Something like that."

"Didn't seem too bright."

"Neither of 'em were what you might call the brains of the operation. You did take care of Aldous, didn't you?"

"Hmm? Aldous? Oh, sure. He was the one driving the Continental, right?"

"No. No, that was Federico."

"Oh," said Rhino. "Well, then... uh... no."

The metallic *click* of the pistol cock caused every spring, wire, and cable in Rhino's body to tense.

"Steady now," rasped a voice from over his shoulder. "Hands up and turn around real slow."

Rhino silently cursed himself for not anticipating a fourth man. Four million, after all, splits four ways. He raised his hands, a lock-pick still held in each, then shuffled around on his knees to face the man limping into the room. He was short and square-shaped, with a gray overcoat and a square head. Rusty exhaust pipes curved up from his cheeks and a single eye of black pearl twinkled under his brow.

"I'm guessing you're Aldous?" said Rhino.

"That's right," the square-head replied. Each time he opened his mouth, a gob of black ink spilled over his bottom lip and dribbled down his shirtfront. "And I already know you... by reputation."

"I got a reputation now?" Rhino asked, cocking an eyebrow.

"As a punk, yeah. As a lunk-headed gun for hire. No mob ties, no contract work, no outstanding affiliations and sure as shit no initiative."

"Ouch," said Rhino.

"Point being," Aldous rocked impatiently back and forth on his heels, "you don't take a job unless it's handed to you on a silver platter with a stack of bills. And yet, less than four hours since we snatch Zigguroth, here you are, paintin' the walls with the blood of my friends and cuttin' my score loose. It would be... *remiss* of me if, before I kill you, I didn't ask: Who in the hell brought you in on this?"

Rhino found himself staring down the barrel of a gun.

"Uh... nobody really," he said. "Not exactly. I mean... it's kind of a weird tale."

Aldous snorted at this, sending plumes of coal-black smoke belching out of his cheek pipes. "Coincidence, is that it?" he snapped. "Gonna tell me it was 'just one of those things?' The hand of freakin' providence?"

"That last one," Rhino said, nodding. "That sounds good."

Aldous had just opened his mouth to say more when Zigguroth's hand came down on him hard. Apparently, it had scaled the wall behind him while he'd been distracted by his own monologue. Digging its file-like nails deep into his metal scalp, the hand then plunged its thumb through his obsidian eye, poking it deep into his oversized toaster of a head.

Aldous screamed as he involuntarily squeezed the trigger, putting two slugs through the ceiling. He stumbled backwards through the door, slapping blindly at the hand as it danced nimbly about his head, punching and clawing at him ferociously. When he tripped down the stairwell and over the handrail, he plummeted seven floors down to the concrete below.

Moments after the deafening *CLAAANG*, the hand strolled back into the room like a lazy crab.

"That's one hell of a thing," said Rhino, regarding the hand in awe.

"Oh yeah," Zigguroth agreed. "Sure is."

***

It took less than four minutes for Rhino to free Caligula Zigguroth from his shackles. One phone call and fifteen minutes later, the platinum-plated pimp was getting examined by his private physician in the back of his own private ambulance, while his private clean-up crew dealt with the broken bodies of the night.

"I really can't thank you enough, Rhino," he said again. "Obviously there will be a monetary payment of some sort to illustrate my gratitude. Truth is... my sons are selfish imbeciles who'd off me themselves if they only had the balls. They'd have never paid a ransom."

Rhino was only half-listening. He was more focused on playing Rock, Scissors, Paper with the hand. The hand was winning by a stretch.

"You really don't need to thank me," he said. "Thank your little friend here. Speaking of which and incidentally, uh... how... I mean... um... *How*?"

Zigguroth smiled. "A little wealth can get you a lot of things in the Grudge, my friend. In addition to all the enemies. You might find this out for yourself one day."

Rhino nodded, though the explanation wasn't entirely to his satisfaction. "Well anyhow," he said. "At least you can reattach it now, I guess."

"No, no, that's quite all right," Zigguroth replied. "I want you to keep it. I can always get more."

"Really?" said Rhino, astonished.

Zigguroth grinned silver. "Really."

The entourage pulled away in their caravan of black limousines, leaving Rhino and the hand on the sidewalk. Checking his watch, Rhino saw it was coming up on 5 a.m. – the same hour the early shift clocked on at Blinky's.

"Breakfast?" he asked.

The hand stuck up its thumb.

Rhino grinned as he took up the slack on the leash. "Lead the way."

And so the two of them started back downtown, passing a few early risers on the way.

They rubbed their eyes and stared after them, almost like they'd never seen a grown man taking a severed hand for a morning stroll.

Gutter Politics

The girl slid into the back seat of the town car, tugging at the hem of her dress like she was afraid she might leave a stain on the upholstery.

Coll waited till she was all the way in and had closed the door behind her, then pulled away from the curb, heading east towards the reservoir.

"This is really somethin,'" the girl said, after they'd driven a few streets in silence. "Feelin' like you're my chauffeur, like I'm some big-name torch singer on her way to the Blanko." Her earrings jangled every time she moved her jaw.

"You never ridden in the back seat before?" Coll asked, his tone humorless.

"Not *alone*," she said, raising an eyebrow. "And when it's just two of us, most johns like me up front with them."

Coll said nothing.

"Sorry," she said, when she'd grown tired of the silence a second time. "I shouldn't talk about other johns. You don't want to hear about that. I can tell. It's just... me and my big mouth."

"Oh really?"

"Yeah, I get teased about it a lot. Y'know, from the other girls. 'Oh, don't tell anything to Vonda,' they'll say, 'She'll blab it all over town.' I'm not stupid, y'know. I'm not, whatever you think."

"That so?"

"Oh, but you don't have anything to worry about. Not at all. Exception made. Seriously, like I says, I'm no moron. I might talk a lot even when I don't mean to, but I'm not an idiot. You can trust me on that." Suddenly she grinned. "Boy oh boy, will you just listen to me? I just can't keep quiet, can I? Y'know, I might actually be a little nervous? How weird is that? Like I've never been picked up by somebody famous before."

Coll kept his gloved hands on the wheel, his eyes fixed on the road ahead.

"I have, y'know," Vonda continued. "Couple of times. I could tell you stories... Not that I ever *would,* y'know. Like I says, I'm not like that. I'm just sayin' I *could.* I could tell you a whole bunch. Some of these guys, like... make out they're Mr. Entertainment, nothin' but joy in their souls, but get 'em in the back room with a few drinks and it's a whole other story, let me tell you. You get used to that being the way. I guess I just never expected somebody like you..."

The car navigated the outskirts of Norrland, heading into the Industrial District.

"I'm not someone to judge," said Vonda, staring out the window. "I mean... we're all people, aren't we? We all have needs, desires... No sense pretending you don't, but I guess you have to, don't you? Got to make out like you're better than everyone else, when you can't be, you *shouldn't have to be*... Must be difficult."

Another minute passed in silence.

Vonda leaned forward. "Y'know, if you're having trouble findin' a spot, there's a motel not too far from here... couple of blocks. The owner gets a cut every week from Mr. Zigguroth, so it won't cost you any extra."

"I've got a place in mind," Coll answered. "We're almost there."

"Okay." She sat back, fingernail tapping against one plastic kneecap. "Okay, sure."

The car passed through one iron gateway, then another, emerging on the other side as the only vehicle on a single lane road in the middle of a square mile of concrete water basins. Halogen lanterns lit their way the first 500 yards, then petered out as they passed a row of low, darkened buildings and slowed to a halt on a wide stretch of gravel.

"You sure know how to pick the romantic spots," Vonda said.

Coll gave her a quick glance in the rear-view – his narrow eyes looking like streaks of burning phosphorous in the gloom – then stepped out of the car. He was opening her door a moment later, offering his hand so she could emerge as gracefully as possible. He kept his eyes on her the whole time, noticing the way her spray-painted smile shivered, betraying the slightest touch of nerves.

She wasn't much to look at, even by Grudge standards, but she carried herself with confidence – a useful trait in her line of work. Her face was her best feature: smooth enamel mask framing bright round eyes and that big mouth she'd mentioned, foam rubber lips concealing uneven but polished copper teeth. She even had freckles, and a beauty spot on her cheek, painted in ever-so-delicate acrylic, but these were the last of her pleasing attributes. The hair on her head was a cheap red wig. Under her chin, a thick neck of interwoven plastic tubes, slick with mucus, led down to a skinny body of oddly-angled alloys, bolts and bone. The faded nylon dress she wore was designed to be revealing, yet revealed far too much.

Standing beside Coll – with his glossy black features, starched white collar and pinstripe suit – she looked even more of a joke.

If the thought had crossed her mind, however, she didn't let it show. Closing the distance between them, she reached out her thin hands and pressed them to his chest, feeling the hard contours of his body beneath the fabric. "You've got every reason to want to be discreet," she said. "I get that. But I think we're alone now." Her fingers inched towards his belt buckle.

"Not here," he said. When his lips moved, they revealed black teeth and a black tongue in a glistening black mouth. "Over here." He took her wrist, enclosing it completely in his hand, and led her past heating buildings and an empty pump station to a rusted metal platform overlooking the reservoir.

"There," he said, waving his arm across the vast expanse of dark water, stretching into the horizon. "Have you ever seen anything like that?"

"No," Vonda answered, the sound of genuine awe unmistakable in her voice. "I've... I've never been here before."

“The Gilberdyke Reservoir,” he said. “This is where it starts. Where the whole city starts. The canals start here. Fester's River. The water for the distilleries, the factories, the power stations... this is it. Over there...” He pointed to a cluster of round buildings. “Those are the clarifiers that prepare the water for drinking. That's where the stuff in your faucet comes from. But over this way is where the real magic happens.”

He led her in the other direction, along the platform and then down, back onto the gravel. She could hear the cacophony of rushing water in the darkness ahead.

“Here,” he called, above the din. “Here we are.” They approached another set of railings at the edge of a huge sloping gutter that had been carved out of the rock. Water churned below them in a frothing stream, disappearing into the mouth of a black tunnel.

“Well?” Vonda laughed, knowing she was supposed to be impressed. “What is it?”

“This,” said Coll, “is the sewer. Point A.”

“Oh...”

“Our sewers are the veins of the city, Vonda,” said Coll. “They keep us alive. And this is where it starts. The water that goes in here is filtered through digesters into the bioreactor, where it's treated with lye, boiled, retreated and purified all before it hits Point B at the corner of 1st and Norrland. The whole process takes about ten minutes. And it's put through all that just so the people of our fair city can shit and piss into it every minute of every day of the week.”

“Really...” said Vonda, sounding short on enthusiasm.

“The point,” said Coll, “is that anything entering here, at Point A, will be utterly pulverized, smashed into microbes of matter, by the time it reaches Point B. Why, if *you* fell in here, that would be it for you. No question about it. In just a few minutes your entire body would be reduced to a chemical soup, diluted and dispersed to a hundred thousand homes. Undetectable, untraceable, *gone*.”

“Wow,” said Vonda, peering down into the froth. “Really?”

"Yeah," Coll said, and shoved her over the rails.

***

"This city. This miserable stinking city..." Regan gripped both sides of the podium and bent his tarnished head to the microphone. "Listen up, you pathetic excuses for men!"

The crowd laughed. Somebody towards the back shouted something indecipherable.

"You better listen to me if you want to save your jobs, save your families, save yourselves!" When Regan yelled, orange sparks flew from his jaw. It wasn't hard to see why he'd been elected ChaBro Co. Union rep and held the position for close to ten years, despite never quite coming out on top in all of his negotiations with management. "This miserable city has taken a lot from us, over the years. Taken our sweat, our time, our blood. Damn near bled us dry it has, and for what? For a little less than a grown man can live on, we've toiled down here in the muck, while the rich get richer... the fat get fatter... and I ache. Deep in my bones I ache." Regan clamped a hand to his stomach, for a moment seized by pain. The crowd in the hall stayed deathly quiet while he composed himself.

"You know all this," he continued, a tremor of sickness in his voice. The growl reverberated back towards him through the speakers. "You don't need me to tell you all this. We've all suffered. What you want is for me to tell you things will get better. Well... I can't promise you that. But what I *can* tell you is that things are going to change. Starting here. Now. Today. In this room. And with the help – I'm not too proud to say it – of a very powerful friend..." He paused there for dramatic effect. Seemed well-placed.

"You've heard me talk long enough," he said. "Gents, without further ado, I give you the next Mayor of Grudgehaven... Eddie Coll!"

The applause as Coll emerged from the wings was thunderous. The five thousand shift jockeys in the hall stamped their iron heels, threw back their heads and bellowed for all they were worth. A part of Coll found it genuinely unnerving, but he tried not to let it show. He shook hands with Regan, patted him on the back, said something complimentary in his ear and sent him on his way, stepping up to the podium like it had been carved for him.

“Thank you,” he said, waving his hands for them to quiet down. “Thank you,” he repeated, till they'd settled back into their seats. “My good friend Jed Regan said something interesting there. He says he can't promise you things will get better. That's the thing about Regan, he's an honest man. He doesn't want to go making promises he can't keep. Gentlemen... *I* will make you that promise. I promise you victory. I promise you justice. I promise you cold hard cash!”

A cheer. The crowd got up on their feet.

“The folks on the hill better get ready,” Coll cried above the rabble. “Our time is now! And we're coming for 'em!”

***

“Nice speech,” Sebastian said to him in the limousine. “You didn't like the one I wrote you?”

“I got inspired,” Coll answered, pouring whiskey into a tumbler. “I like a passionate audience.”

“They were that,” said Sebastian. “Too passionate to notice the part where you called yourself a liar.”

Coll took a deep drink from the glass before replying. “I did what now?”

“All that stuff about promises. 'Regan here, he's too honest to make a promise he can't keep, but me? I'll say whatever I damn well please...'”

Coll waved his hand dismissively. “That's not what I said.”

“Close enough,” said Sebastian. “Truth is you don't know what you said.”

“They knew what I meant.” Coll loosened his tie and undid the top button of his shirt. His fingertips left ink-black smears on everything they touched.

“Maybe they did. But you've got to be careful. Off-the-cuff rhetoric might play fine to the Dusties, but one of Morrow's men gets a hold of a quote like that, they'll pick it to pieces."

Coll smirked and took another sip. "Morrow's men... And where are all Morrow's men?"

"You've got 'em all too scared to come south of Septicemia," Sebastian said, unable to resist a smile. "Think they'll get scalped for their gold plating. Which is not to say that nobody's been paying attention to you." He reached under his seat and produced a briefcase, then handed it across. "From the King of Eyes. A 'contribution to your campaign.'"

Coll raised an eyebrow, though it was hard to tell. His features were difficult to make out even in the brightest light. He popped the locks on the case and eased it open, finding it full of crisp notes. "Shouldn't you be keeping hold of this?"

"Can't." Sebastian shook his head. "We can't have donations from known gangsters on the books. And it'd be suicide to try to give it back, so... enjoy, I guess. Treat your wife. Or... whomever." There was that smile again.

Coll peered out through the window, up at the sky, imagining he could sense one of the King's airships passing overhead. The King of Eyes was rumored to have a fleet, ferrying him and his men between the spires of the Grudge's tallest buildings. The stories said they were painted black and stripped of lights, so as to appear invisible against the clouds that hung permanently over the city.

"Did he say what he wanted for it?" Coll asked.

"Nothing. I think it's a genuine donation. You've earned his approval and he wants to help you out. God help him, but I think he actually believes in you."

Coll closed the case, sat back in the seat and drained his glass. "Sucker," he said.

***

The phone was already ringing when Coll entered his office. Kicking the door closed and dropping the briefcase onto a chair, he crossed to the desk and picked it up. “Hello?”

“Is this Councilman Eddie Coll?” The voice was slow, mannered.

“Yes. Who's this?”

“I know what you did, Eddie.”

“I beg your pardon?”

“I know... what you did.”

Coll was silent for a moment. “You'll, uh, have to be more specific.”

“The hooker, Eddie. At the reservoir. I saw what you did to her. You're a bad, bad boy, Eddie. A bad boy.”

“I, uh... I don't know what you're talking about.”

“Sure you don't. I didn't think you would. But that's okay. It'll come to you. This was just a courtesy call, anyway. To let you know that I know. I'll give you some time to think it over. Then we can talk properly.”

“Wait.”

“Goodbye for now, Councilman.”

“Wait a sec...”

He heard a click, and the crackle of a dead line. Before he was even aware it was happening, his hands had slammed the receiver down, picked it back up and dialed his secretary.

“Yes, Councilman Coll?”

“June,” he said. “That call you just put through here. Where did it come from?”

“I'm sorry, sir. I didn't put anyone through. It must have been direct. I'm sure if it's important they'll call back.”

“Direct. Yes. Thank you.”

He hung up and sank slowly down into his chair. A direct line meant internal. It meant the caller had been using a government phone.

***

The modest Midtown apartment Coll shared with his wife was more commensurate with the official living he made as an elected representative of the people than with the magnificent wealth he'd amassed from bribes, underhanded deals and plain old-fashioned theft, but it at least offered wonderful views of the South-Western Quarter.

Glass of whiskey clutched in his hand, dark smear on the rim, he stood at the window, staring across the battlemented towers of 28th Street and past the railway bridge, to the pulsing neon hub still referred to by some of the older gentry as 'Paramour Park.'

A visit tonight, he knew, was in all probability a bad idea. And yet...

He saw Lilith's reflection in the glass as she approached. He couldn't see his own – his bald, black head didn't reflect enough light for that – but he saw her silver form as she prowled through the darkness towards him, not making a sound. It was eerie, the way she did that. She was a sleek and eerie woman.

"Rough day at the office," she sighed, slipping her slender arms about his waist and pressing her cheek to his shoulder.

"It wasn't so bad," he replied.

"I was talking about me," she said.

"Oh."

Her legs coiled their way effortlessly around his, knitted steel fibers twisting like a knot of snakes. Her neck stretched, giving out only the slightest groan as it did, and her head slid over his shoulder and around, meeting him face-to-face.

"Sometimes I wonder," she said, through pursed green lips, "If I'm really cut out to be a Mayor's wife."

Coll gazed into her mirrored eyes, seeing only his own reflection. "You'd be great,” he saw himself say. “But you shouldn't worry. It's a long way off a certainty.”

Her hand appeared at his collar, elongated fingers brushing softly against his cheek. His skin oozed over them, coating them thickly at the slightest touch. When they came away they looked like they'd been dipped in tar. “

I'm going to bed,” she told him, confirming what he'd already guessed. The touch had been a less-than-subtle clue. She was careful only to touch his skin when they were alone together, no other appointments for the day. Whenever they made love she ended up painted in his grease. Such images were best kept out of the public eye.

“You go ahead,” he told her. “I have to go out. I'll only be a couple hours.”

“Fine,” she said, and kissed his cheek, turning her green lips black. Then she untangled herself from around him and slithered away to the bedroom.

Not one question about where he was going or why. *Yeah,* he thought. *One hell of a Mayor's wife.*

***

Paramour Park's unofficial borders were Gonorrhea and Chancroid, between 30th and 32nd. Easing his automobile around the corner of Gonorrhea and 30th, Coll was hit with a wall of dancing light. The cars ahead of him inched forward like they were moving through treacle, while their drivers perused the advertised attractions of the bordellos and the displayed wares of the girls on the sidewalk.

“LIVE SHOWS DAILY” said one arrangement of sizzling pink bulbs. “GAMBLING! DANCING! GIRLS!” said another. A few yards along the boulevard the signage became more overt, the younger establishments battling to assert themselves with claims of “WILD SEX ACTS”, “CHEAP, LEWD THRILLS” and “EXOTIC, NASTY, CRAZY LADIES.” Coll's personal favorite was a fluorescent sculpture, lit from within, detailing an especially buxom broad who appeared to be one half woman and one half octopus. The flickering yellow sign beneath simply read: “WEIRD SHIT.”

The erring sisters on the street, for their part, did their best to live up to the expectations those signs cultivated. Born and raised in the Grudge's worst slums, ravaged by drugs and disease, then beaten into a life of bondage, they were ferociously ugly creatures all peddling a fantasy of sensuality and glamor. The contradiction made for some arresting imagery – iron rivets poking through fishnet stockings; body glitter smeared over cauterized sinew; leatherette lips fixed into place by wire and staples... The johns who came here would pay anyway.

For Coll – and these ladies – tonight was not the night. Paramour Park was too busy, too excited, too brightly lit for his purposes. He enjoyed the parade while it lasted, then drove on, a few streets over, turning south on 35th, where the pleasures of Paramour were still on offer, though not as overtly. There were still girls here, but neither they – nor any flashing bright lights – were making any promises they couldn't keep.

Coll drove along the curb to where one broad stood, her thin and jagged body lit only by the glow of a nearby trash fire. She was completely bald and, when she bent down to his window, Coll saw that her eyes, too, were aflame. Thin fingers of orange and red danced in the sockets.

“Ten for mouth stuff,” she said, her voice as rough as sandpaper. “Twenty below the waist. Thirty for the works.”

Coll dipped into his pocket and held up a $100 bill. “Get in the back,” he said.

***

Kellie – that was her name – wasn't quite the easy mark Vonda had been. She'd only been in the back seat a few moments before Coll realized her beautiful flaming eyes were lit by a coal fire in her skull. Every few minutes she took a briquette from her purse and slid it in through the grate at the back of her head. He had to roll all the windows down because of the smoke.

She also didn't seem nearly so eager to please as Vonda, quick to anger when they sped up into Midtown and onto Norrland Avenue, heading

East towards the reservoir.

“Where the hell d'you think you goin'?” she spat. “I can't be all night with this! I gots places to be! You didn't say nothin' bout no cross-town trip! My boy Herriot'll be hot white rage he hears about this!”

He threw a few more bills over his shoulder to quiet her down, but that didn't last long.

Heading into the industrial sector she hit the roof, wanting no part of any “funny, weird-ass, creepy, kinky, shadowy shit” he had planned.

Coll, reluctantly, was forced to submit, making a U-turn at 5th and heading back the way they'd come, then dipping into an alley in the middle of the Entertainment District. It was a risky place to be turning tricks. Riskier still to be committing murder, but that's where he did it.

A forced smile on his lips and a knife hidden up his sleeve, he slipped into the back seat beside her, put his arms around her and slid the knife in between her ribs. She made an odd squeaking sound in her throat and he heard something like the snap of a hinge in her head, before the fire in her eyes went out.

When she was safely concealed on the floor of his car, Coll drove out of the alley and back onto Norrland, following it all the way to the reservoir.

Arriving a little after midnight, he helped Kellie up the steps to the platform and gave his usual speech – such was his custom – then back down and over to the foaming mouth of the sewer.

“Why, if *you* fell in here,” he said, resting her lifeless head against his shoulder. “That would be it for you. No question about it. In just a few minutes your entire body would be reduced to a chemical soup, diluted and dispersed to a hundred thousand homes. Undetectable, untraceable, *gone*.”

“Wow,” he said, out the side of his mouth, moving Kellie's jaw with his finger. “That sure is interesting, Councilman Coll. And might I just say, I think that you would make a most excellent mayor of Grudgehaven.” It was a poor imitation of her voice.

"Thank you, Kellie. I'm glad you think so," he said, and shoved her over.

***

The next day Sebastian met him in his office with the news that Gunnar and Eagleton had both withdrawn their candidacies.

"Why would they do that?" Coll asked, stunned.

"The King of Eyes." Sebastian grinned, pouring them both a drink from the cocktail cabinet in the corner. "The word has filtered down that you're his man. You're the one he wants. He already owns a third of all the ward bosses in the city, so neither Gunnar or Eagleton would've stood a chance. Now they've done the sensible thing and allied themselves with you. Hopefully their voters will do the same." He held out a glass, brimming with amber liquid.

Coll took it. "I can't do the math. Where does this leave us with Morrow?"

Sebastian swallowed, liquor spilling down his chin. "He's still ahead, with Broken Glass in his corner. But the gap is closing."

The King of Broken Glass was the Grudge's second great crime lord. He and the King of Eyes had been waging a bitter, evenly-matched war of attrition against each other for as long as anyone in the city could remember.

"I can't believe this," Coll said.

"I've never seen anything like it," Sebastian admitted. "It's you, Ed. I always said you had a natural talent. A God-given gift for politics. Now we just need to get you up-to-speed with the nuts and bolts, the cold facts, get you a few razor-sharp *arguments* to go with all that militant oratory of yours and we'll be able to hand Morrow his own ass on a platter. The miserable old queen..."

Coll's phone rang. He picked it up. "Hello?"

"You did it again. I can't believe you did it again!"

Coll said nothing for a moment, painfully aware of Sebastian just a few feet away. “I beg your pardon?”

“The hooker! Another one! What, did you think I was kidding when I called you up yesterday? Did you think I was just guessing? What's the matter with you? You are sick, Coll. Y'hear me? You're a sick, sick, freak and it is about time somebody held you to account. Your twisted little hobby is gonna cost you big, Councilman. Y'hear me? It's gonna cost you big time!”

Coll placed the receiver to his chest and said to Sebastian: “Sorry, Seb. I have to take this. Can you give me five minutes?”

Sebastian nodded, his lips at the whiskey glass, and headed for the door, pausing briefly on his way out to point at the briefcase on the chair and ask: “Is that what I think it is? Eddie, you need to do something about that.”

“Don't worry,” Coll said. “I've got it in hand.” The door pulled shut and Coll put the receiver back to his ear. “Go on,” he said.

“I want ten thousand,” the voice said. “For starters. Ten thousand in cash to keep my mouth shut till the election's over.”

“How about two hundred thousand?” Coll said. “And I never hear from you again.”

“...that could work.”

“Midnight. Tonight. The Reservoir. Come alone.”

“You too,” the voice said. “And don't try anything clever. Just remember – I'm watching you.” Again the line clicked and went dead.

Coll put the receiver down and stared for several seconds at the King of Eyes' briefcase, then picked the phone back up and placed a call to the Sanitation Department's head office.

***

Stepping out of the car onto the gravel, Coll could sense something had changed. The vibrations under his feet were different. The industrial noise of the facility around him was missing some vital component. He was so finely tuned to its rhythms that it only took him a moment's concentration to catch the missing piece, then he was moving, quickly, briefcase in hand, to the mouth of the sewer.

When he peered over the railings he saw the trench into which he'd thrown the bodies was dry. An electric gate had been raised out of the ground to dam the flow from the reservoir. No torrent of water to churn anyone into soup and filter them through the digesters. Just a gaping wound in the rock.

“I thought I better shut it down just to be on the safe side.”

Coll turned towards the voice and spied a squat, lumpen form strolling towards him through the shadows.

“In case you maybe got it in your head to throw me in there.”

As he drew nearer, Coll saw the man wore a wide-brimmed fedora, pulled down, and a wax-treated raincoat, collar turned up, doing his best to obscure his face.

“It would be a lie to say the thought hadn't crossed my mind,” Coll admitted.

“Yeah, well... this is in case you get any other dangerous thoughts.” The little man raised his arm and Coll saw he was holding a small black revolver.

“You don't need that,” Coll said.

“Let's hope not,” the man answered. The two were now only a couple feet apart. “You got the money?”

Coll held up the briefcase.

“Open it,” the man ordered, making a neat little movement with his gun.

Coll knelt, set the case down and did as he was asked, revealing two perfect rows of stacked, bound $50 bills.

“That's... okay, that's good,” the man said. The excitement in his voice was unmistakable. “Now... take 'em all out the case and stack 'em up. I want to see the case empty. Make sure you've not snuck anything else in there, like a bomb or whatever."

"Really?" Coll groaned.

"Shaddap. Do what I say."

Coll took the stacks out one at a time, till the case was empty, then picked it up, turned it over and shook it. "Satisfied?" "Yeah, that's good. You can put 'em all back in. But flick through 'em when you do. I wanna make sure you ain't tried to fool me with real bills taped to stacks of blank paper."

Coll sighed. "This is taking longer than I thought it would." Again, he did what the man wanted, going through one stack at a time, his thumb leaving little smudges of black on the corners. When the full $200,000 was back in the case he snapped it closed, grabbed the handle and stood. "Well? Are we good?"

"Oh yeah." The man sounded like he was salivating. Beneath the brim of his hat his eyes glowed red, trained on the case. "Yeah, we're good."

"Good," Coll said, and tossed the case into the trench.

"No!" The man screamed, throwing his body against the rail and thrusting out his free hand towards the case as it spun away from him. His left foot lifted up as he stretched, making a desperate, futile grab at the air.

Coll saw the foot as it came up, snatched it around the ankle and heaved the man all the way over the rail. Screaming, he plummeted twenty feet down to the cement floor, landing with a *CRACK* so loud that it echoed.

Coll took a deep breath, enjoying the all-too-brief period of silence that followed. The briefcase had split when it landed, setting free a cloud of bills that whirled and danced in the breeze from the reservoir.

His blackmailer moaned, pathetically. "My back... My freakin' back..."

Coll peered over the railing and clasped his hands together. "How're you feeling, Hugo? You don't mind me calling you Hugo, do you?"

"Oh God..." The squat man writhed on the ground, a puddle of thin slime oozing out the back of his hatless head. His eyes were spots of dull color in a face of cracked brown slate and pus.

"Hugo Yorki," Coll said. "Fluoridation tech for the sanitation department, assigned these past couple nights to detail the clarifiers. The only man working this section. How easy do you think it was for me to get that information, Hugo?"

"Damn you," Hugo spat. "Son of a bitch."

"That's right. Real easy. See, you put the wind up me with that first call, I'll admit that. But last night? I was very careful to make sure I wasn't being followed, so for you to have seen anything meant you already had to be here, on site, just a few hundred yards away. And you called me from a government phone, which had to mean Sanitation. Then all I had to do to get your name, age, weight and job title was make a phone call. You getting how easy you made this? I hate to break it to you, Hugo, but you're not a very smart man."

Hugo's heels started to kick, like he was beginning to work some feeling back into his legs.

"You're an opportunist," Coll continued. "I can respect that. But I'm telling you all this because I think you made some very stupid assumptions about me. Assumptions that need to be corrected."

Now water began to pour into the trench – not from the reservoir, but from the sewer. Foaming brown liquid poured in a lazy stream over the lip of the tunnel and began to spread uphill towards Hugo.

"First off," said Coll. "You're wrong if you think I care about my political career. If I'm mayor this time next year, that's just dandy, but as far as I'm concerned *that's* the hobby, understand? My *job* is to feed the sewer. That's who I am and it's what I do. I'm not some depraved psycho-sexual serial killer. I don't get my kicks doing this. I do it because it *needs* to be done!"

The water swelled around Hugo now, soaking through his clothes. He rolled onto his side and started to pull himself onto his feet.

"The sewer is alive, Hugo," said Coll. "She's the living, breathing soul of this city. She's a protector, a provider and a mother. And when she could no longer sustain herself on the dregs you and your miserable kind offered her, she did the incredible. She gave birth to a son."

Hugo, shrieking in fear and confusion, raised the pistol and fired twice.

The bullets struck Coll square in the chest, exploding out through his back. He didn't flinch.

"Now what did I say about that, Hugo?" he said. "What have I just been telling you? I'm a man made of concentrated shit, Hugo. What, exactly, did you think bullets were going to do to me?"

Hugo, dumbfounded, dropped the revolver and ran up the slope to the gate, trying to claw his way up its smooth iron surface.

Coll shook his head. "You just don't listen, do you? That's what I really hate about you and your kind. First order of business when I'm elected, I'm going to clean up the Sanitation Department. She deserves better than you."

The water was up to Hugo's knees now, frothing sewage lapping against the back of his thighs. He screamed, pounding on the gate, and would have gone on screaming and pounding had a claw of glistening black effluent not shot up out of the water, seized him by the neck and pulled him under.

Hugo fought for as long as he could. Coll watched his body as it was carried downhill, sucked towards the mouth of the sewer by the current. He thrashed violently in the water, lashing out with his arms and legs at more dark shapes as they swam in to restrain him. When he was less than a foot from entering the tunnel his head resurfaced, eyes and mouth popped wide. He managed to let out the shortest of screams before black tentacles speared upwards from the water and swarmed into his throat. Then he was gone.

Coll watched the waters recede for a while, taking with them all trace of the fluoridation tech and the money, then went in search of a switch to lower the reservoir gate. He knew that, when she finished her meal, Mom would want a drink to wash the taste away.

***

Lilith slapped him awake with a wet towel. She was fresh from the shower and didn't want to put her hands on him.

“What is it?” Coll moaned.

“Sebastian,” she said, holding out the phone.

He sat up in bed, wearily rubbing the sleep from his eyes, and put the receiver to his ear. “Yeah?”

“You asleep?” Sebastian's tinny voice demanded to know.

“I've been having a lot of late nights.”

“You've not been listening to the news?”

“No. Why? What is it?”

Sebastian took a brief pause before he said it. “The King of Broken Glass is dead.”

Coll sat up straight, his eyes widening, grip tightening on the phone. “What?”

“It was a hit. The King of Eyes took out him and his entire convoy in the Garment District. Huge ambush. He wiped them out. Game over.”

“I can't believe it.”

“No one can. It's on every station. End of an era. Eyes has it. He's got the city.”

“What does this mean... for us?”

Sebastian laughed. “Well, for starters, it means you're going to regret some of the promises you made those union boys. It means you can afford to move out of Midtown. Means we're drinking champagne only for the next month. Get dressed. I'm coming over there.”

“Wait. You're serious. You're serious?”

“Buddy, he *owns* the Grudge! That's how big this is. And you're his boy. For better or worse, he's picked you. Mayor Eddie Coll.”

***

Coll got the call to meet with Mayor Wyndam Morrow two days later. The word had come down from on high. With the election still six months away, the King of Eyes had decided Coll had already won. He was to move into the office and take control with immediate effect. Morrow would be allowed to keep the title till polling day, but that was all it was. A title.

When Coll met him in his office he was already packed up. He sat at his desk, surrounded by boxes, staring into the bottom of a glass of scotch. He wouldn't even look at Coll, but when he spoke, every word was laced with contempt.

“You think it'll be easy,” Morrow sneered. “You don't have the first idea.” He had a puffed-up, triangular head with tiny black eyes and a tiny black mouth. Coll was amazed he'd ever found the man impressive. From where he was standing he looked like a misshapen marshmallow in a suit.

“Slime, filth and misery,” Morrow said, turning his back to Coll, staring out of the window. “That's all this job is, whatever ideals you have, whatever dreams you may hold of transforming it. Step behind this desk and your life becomes one endless river of *stinking shit*. You really think you got what it takes?”

Coll had to laugh.

Down to the Bones

"Apologies to anyone tuning in for the GBC Mystery Theater. This station is now broadcasting comprehensive extreme weather coverage and will be doing so until the storm has passed. Once again, forecasters are predicting a city-wide Category 5 acid rainfall within the hour. All listeners are advised to get indoors and stay there until further notice. If you have property in the street, you can protect it with an acid-resistant tarp as provided to most homes by City Hall. If you do not have a tarp, please do not put yourself at risk by trying to get one. If your home has been left uncovered or has not been treated for acid rainfall within the last five years, please notify emergency services immediately. I'm joined in the studio by rainfall expert Dr. Peatree Witheroe. Thank you for joining us, Dr. Witheroe."

"It's my pleasure, Dan."

"Doc, it seems like just yesterday the two of us were in this very studio under these exact same circumstances. I can't believe it was nearly three years ago, can you?"

"No, I can hardly believe it myself, Dan."

"I'd wager both you and I – and indeed many of the listeners at home – are old enough to recall a time when a Category 5 rainfall was viewed as... well, as a once-in-a-lifetime meteorological event. Now it seems to befall our fair city with frightening regularity."

"That's correct, yes. In fact, our records show that the periods between rainfalls have dramatically reduced with each passing storm."

"You mean to say that next time could be just two years away? Or one year?"

"Quite possibly, yes."

"How do you account for that, Doc?"

"Well, there is vigorous debate within the scientific community. A lot of my colleagues have their own pet theories. Personally, I believe the weather is simply reacting to the tremendous changes we've unthinkingly made to our own atmosphere in the last couple of decades."

"You're referring to the industrial downturn?"

"I am, Dan. Put simply, we're just not burning fuel like we used to. Factories are closing down, chimneys being bricked up... The chemical emissions that would once have balanced out the naturally-occurring acid in our atmosphere simply aren't there any more. Take Old Town as an example. Once, it was a thriving manufacturing hub, generating a clean, healthy smog. Now it's close to empty and being overtaken more and more by encroaching Blacklands vegetation, which produces harmful chemicals of its own. Added to which, my own studies have shown that almost every instance of serious acid rainfall in the last two decades has been immediately preceded by a period of industrial action."

"Then you're laying the blame on the ChaBro strikers?"

"Well, I'd rather not be drawn into any political debates, Dan. I'm a man of science."

"Of course. As a man of science then, what can you tell us about this rain in particular?"

"I can tell you that it's highly corrosive and will eat through almost anything, whether it's organic matter, rock, metal... If you were to place a block of solid steel – four feet by four by four – on the ground and allow a single raindrop to fall on it, that raindrop would burn through, all the way down, the full four feet."

"That sounds like powerful stuff."

"Oh, it is. I think most everyone in Grudgehaven is used to enduring a little acid rain, but not like this. You'd have more chance of surviving a hail of bullets than a Category 5."

"Well let's hope that's not next. You said the rain could eat through almost *anything. Can you expand on that?"*

"Certainly. There are certain substances and compounds that are acid-resistant. Glass, for example, certain plastics, certain fibers... Obviously, there are the tarps and treating agents mass-produced by the government. And statistically, one in every 200 Grudgehaven residents is believed to have a natural, in-built resistance to the rain, though most never find out. On balance I'd say it's not worth taking the risk."

"Dr. Witheroe, thank you."

"Thank you."

"Once again, this is Dan Dorian at the GBC Radio Center bringing you up-to-date coverage of the extreme acid rainstorm expected to hit within the hour. We'll have more from Dr. Witheroe later in the show. Right now I'd like to welcome our second guest, Captain Elmo Pazzano of the Grudgehaven Police Department, who's going to be speaking about the dramatic increase in homicides which is expected whenever one of these storms hits and what can be done to combat that. Captain Pazzano, welcome to the show..."

Dana reached for the dial and turned the radio off. She didn't need some smug cop telling her things she already knew. Statistically, more people had been killed during the last Category 5 rainstorm than at any other time in the past three years. It was the same story with the storm before that and it was nothing to do with people getting caught in the rain. What a Category 5 did – quite by accident – was clear the streets of witnesses, scare away the cops and provide a uniquely effective way to dispose of a body. In effect, a Category 5 provided the perfect conditions for murder.

Most of the deaths were mob-related. A storm such as the one about to hit was viewed as a brief "open season" between gangsters – the ideal time to settle scores. However, a high number of domestic murders bulked up the figures, with the wives of abusive husbands, neighbors of anti-social louts and money-hungry nephews of rich, old uncles all looking to get in on the action.

Dana knew all about the now-traditional "Acid Rain Massacres." She'd done her reading and had a murder of her own to commit. She didn't need Captain Pazzano getting in her head and giving her second thoughts.

With the radio switched off the house was eerily quiet, reminding her of why she'd put it on in the first place. Though the drawing room looked as immaculate as ever, she picked the feather duster back up and repeated her patrol, eager to be doing something rather than nothing and gradually working her way over to the bay window. Mercurio Lane was a rich neighborhood, where the narrow, elegant town-houses were stacked closely together and across from each other in neat little rows. All the windows in the street were complemented by exterior iron shutters, all of which were now drawn – except her own. Peering into the street she saw it was empty of people and moving cars. All automobiles were parked and acid-protected. The storm hadn't reached Uptown yet and wasn't due for an hour, but a light drizzle was already falling – the kind of greasy spatters one expected of an evening in the Grudge. Dana stood and watched for a while, hypnotized by the way the raindrops fell through the gray lamplight.

She was startled out of her meditations by the bell at the servant's entrance.

***

"Aren't you going to invite me in?" He was a black silhouette in the doorway. His rain-soaked hat and overcoat glistened in the glow of the lantern over his shoulder, but his face was a mystery in shadow. Only when he raised his head, the brim of his hat revealing two bright, glowing eyes of blue, would she admit to herself it was really him. "You okay, baby?"

"Yes," she answered, through quivering lips. "I just... I had myself convinced you wouldn't show."

"That there sounds like crazy talk." He stepped across the threshold and put his arm around her, pulling her close. "But don't you worry 'bout a thing. Clancy's here now."

She was blinded by his shadow, sensing him only by taste and touch as they embraced. His coiled wire tongue sliced against her own, his mouth oozing warm saliva the flavor of martinis and motor oil. His hard shell lips were as cold and sharp as his cheeks, hands, arms and chest, but she knew a place where his body was soft.

Her delicate fingers moved instinctively to the round aperture in his abdomen, tracing its polished brass outline and feeling the movement of hot air from within, before it reached out for her. The tip of his wet tentacle first tickled her palm, then slid between her fingers, curling over the back of her hand and shocking her skin with the slightest touch of electricity. She gasped, breaking the kiss, as more of its twisting length eased out from his torso, winding its way around her arm and clutching her tight. The sensation sent a shiver of pleasure rippling through her body and, as she stepped back, then fell, wilting, into his eager arms, she found herself wondering again how she had ever hoped to love a man who *wasn't* half-squid.

“Clancy, please,” she breathed, face pressed against his chest. “He'll be home soon. We have to prepare.”

“Sure thing, baby doll.” His smile was a razor of light in the darkness. “Why don't you start by mixing me a drink?”

She hesitated. “You smell like you've already had a few.”

The smile dimmed, just a touch. “I might have had one at the club before they closed up. For courage.”

She gazed up at him, serene and serious. “Did it work?”

“It got me about half-way. It's... a hell of a thing, y'know.”

Her answer was a soft whisper. “I know.”

Dana closed the door behind him as he shook off his coat and hat, then led him upstairs and fixed him a fresh martini. He drank it in the study, where the shutters were closed and the lamps burned low. When he'd drained the glass, he set it down on the mantel, wiped his mouth with the sleeve of his checkered jacket and asked: “Where's the gun?”

“In the desk. Top drawer. He keeps it loaded, so be careful.”

“I know how to handle a loaded gun.” He went around the side of the desk, opened the drawer and lifted out a pearl-handled semi-automatic. “Nice piece. Where's the note?”

Dana slid two fingers into her brassiere and produced a folded sheet of yellow paper. “Here,” she said, holding it out.

“How the hell did you get him to write it?” he asked, pinching it from her hand.

“I didn’t have to. He did it himself. Must have been about four years ago now. Came in drunk, angry, looking to start trouble... Only time I ever saw him like that.” She shivered.

Clancy held out a pack of smokes. She took one. “Go on,” he said, snapping open an enamel lighter.

“All of a sudden he changed.” She touched the cigarette to the flame and sucked fresh smoke into her lungs. “Went all limp, sad and sorry. More like himself. He left me alone, then went and sat down at the desk, wrote the note, put the pistol to his head... and passed out. I found him that way.”

“Four years?” said Clancy. “You kept the note four years?”

“It seemed... prudent,” she breathed. Smoke wound in thin wisps around her head.

“Just how long have you been planning this?”

She smiled and looked him up and down. “All my life. I was just waiting for the right man to come along, y'know?”

Clancy stared at her hard for a moment, then turned his gaze on the note in his hand.

Dearest Grudgehaven, it read. *This charade has gone on long enough. I can't take the pretense or the guilt. I tried not to be who I am but I can't be anyone else and if no one else is willing to put me down, then I need to do it myself. I'm sorry. Signed, the man you knew as Buckshaw.*

“It's dramatic,” said Clancy. “God help me, I almost feel sorry for him.”

“So did I, once,” Dana sighed. “When you break it down all he ever had going for him was cash and sympathy. And sympathy... It passes.”

“You don't have to convince me, baby. I'm with you all the way.”

Dana wasn't listening. “If I thought a divorce was the way... If I thought he'd let me walk out of here with more than the clothes on my back, believe me, I'd do it. He cares too much about the money for that. It's all he really loves. I suppose we've got that much in common.” She sucked hard at the cigarette, wetness gleaming in the corners of her eyes. “God... I used to think I could love him once.”

“Hey.” Clancy grabbed her by the arm and pulled her in towards him, bending his angular face towards hers. “None of that. Don't go soft on me, y'hear? You’ve done the best you can for the guy. You have. But he's not worth it. You've got to worry about your own future. *Our* future. He's all that's standing in our way and even *he* knows he needs to be put down. He said it himself. This is the simplest way. The *best* way. Just you remember that.”

“Sorry,” she sniffed.

“Don't be sorry. And don't be scared.” He grinned. “It's only murder.”

***

The Packard's engine purred like a dozing lion as it rolled into the driveway. The obese man who stepped out wore a sable coat that covered his entire body – all except his burnished copper head. He let himself in the door, checked his pocket watch and barked: “Dana, honey! I need the tarp!”

“I'm in the study, sweetheart,” she called.

“What was that?” Buckshaw stomped down the hallway. “I said I need the tarp. For the car. It's about to start coming down out there.” He turned through the doorway into the study and found his wife calmly mixing bourbon and vermouth.

“Oh, I'm sure there's plenty of time,” she said. “Why don't you take your coat off and have a drink?”

Buckshaw's tiny eyes blinked furiously behind his spectacles. “I... No, thank you. Not right now. I said I need the tarp. Where is it?”

Dana flicked her head towards the desk. “Over there. On the floor.”

The puzzlement deepened on Buckshaw's broad face as he moved across the room. “What's it doing over here?” He found the tarp spread out across the carpet by his desk. Moving the chair out of his way to get at it, his eyes fell upon the note laid flat. “What's this?” Sinking into the chair, he picked the note up and stared at it, taking in its contents and slowly recalling its composition. “Dana?” She kept her back turned to him. “Dana, what's going on?”

The closet door on Buckshaw's right swung open and Clancy stepped out. Buckshaw saw his own pistol clutched in the big man's fist. “This is what's going on, pal.”

Dana said nothing, but her eyes were wide with fear.

Buckshaw looked from Clancy to her, then back to Clancy. His spectacled eyes quit their blinking and hardened as a jagged smile spread across his face. “Oh, you idiots are making a *big* mistake.”

Clancy thrust the pistol into Buckshaw's face.

Dana screamed. “Clancy, don't!”

He squeezed the trigger and blew a hole through the fat man's head. Buckshaw toppled backwards with the chair, dark blood spraying across the tarp.

Clancy watched the gun-smoke as it hung in the air for several seconds, then slowly drifted upwards. When his ears had ceased ringing, he turned to Dana and growled: “What the hell d'you mean *Clancy, don't*?”

Dana's hands were over her mouth. The glass tumbler she'd been carrying lay at her feet, ice scattered across the carpet. “I panicked,” she replied, voice dry as timber. “I'm sorry. It's just... I've never seen him like that before. The way he looked at us... I got scared.”

“Well pull yourself together,” he said, placing the gun down on the desk and throwing off his jacket. “We ain't done yet. Not by a country mile.”

***

They rolled the body up in the tarp and dragged it outside to the driveway. Then they rolled him out of the tarp and threw it – blood side up – over the Plymouth and ran back indoors to await the big show. The idea was for Dana to call the cops in the morning, make out like she'd just discovered the note and was afraid her wealthy, terminally depressed husband had walked out of the house into the Big Bad Rain. The way the acid worked, there likely wouldn't be any remains, but any that turned up would only lend credence to her story and make it that much easier to have him declared dead.

Now they stood at the window, waiting for the storm, almost looking forward to seeing his bloated body reduced to a bubbling puddle of chemicals, washed away into the gutter. It was only after checking the sixth dozenth time that Dana was struck by a terrible thought: "What if it's a mistake?"

"Hmm?" said Clancy. He was staring at the other houses in the street, watching to make sure none opened their shutters. Last thing they needed was a witness.

"What if they got it wrong? About the storm? You know what weathermen are like. What if it doesn't even hit?"

"It'll hit," Clancy assured her. "Just relax. Any second now."

"It should have started ten minutes ago."

"On the south side. That's what they said. It's moving north, so it'll be here any second. Check the radio if you don't believe me. They'll tell you the same."

"No. I can't. I can't! Oh God, Clancy, what have we done?"

"Baby, if you don't calm right now I swear I'll slap you so hard you'll... look."

Her head was in her hands, shaking left and right. "I can't take it."

"Look, God damn it!"

"I can't. I can't..."

"Dana, *look!*"

Reluctantly, she turned her head back towards the window and saw the first fat drops of acid rain as they landed in the driveway. They sizzled and steamed wherever they hit. "Oh thank God," Dana moaned. "Thank you, God..."

The first raindrop to hit Buckshaw's body took him square in the chest. It burned a smoking hole through his sable coat and churned his stretched skin into a bubbling froth. Another hit his thigh, searing through it like a bullet.

"It's working," Clancy said. "See? What'd I tell you?"

In seconds the spatter became a deluge – a gray sheet of acid washing across the street. Clancy and Dana watched as Buckshaw's body was coated and instantly began to collapse on itself, melting into hissing clumps of unrecognizable matter. The coat evaporated in a flash. His seething skin peeled back to reveal a tangle of tubes, wires and white fat that quickly foamed into liquid. His head crumbled up like a cube of sugar dropped in hot coffee. In a matter of moments his whole body was lost behind a funnel of noxious smoke.

His murderers maintained their composure throughout. No gagging, no weeping, no turning away. They wanted to see it through together. Dana stepped closer to Clancy, who put his arm around her shoulder. Her hand slid around his bare back as she leaned her head towards him.

"I don't know what to feel," she sighed.

"Try not to think too hard," Clancy said. "Just be glad it's over."

"Yes," she smiled, seeing the reflection of the two of them in the glass. Then she frowned. "Wait. What's that?"

When the cloud of fumes lifted, the most either of them expected to see was a puddle of sludge. A sad, wet stain that had once been a sad, fat man. Instead, the departing curtain of gases revealed a spread of glistening red bones.

The skeleton that lay in the drive was skinny, with a small rib-cage and slanting, narrow skull. Not what either might have expected from Buckshaw. The bones shone with a fine finish, almost like they'd been lacquered with something, and were utterly resistant to the rain, which pelted off the surface like harmless water. Strangest of all, the skeleton looked to be shorter than Buckshaw by a full foot.

“The bones...” Dana moaned. “His bones aren't melting.”

“That's okay.” Clancy spoke through gritted teeth. “Doesn't change a thing. Not a damn thing. So they find his bones, so what? It's fine.”

Dana pulled away from him. “You shot him in the head, Clancy! What do you think the cops will say when they see the bullet hole in his skull?”

“Will you quit getting hysterical every other second? All we have to do is get rid of the bones. That's easy. We just wait till the.... Wait...” He let the sentence trail off, staring out the glass.

“What do you mean?” Dana demanded. “Wait till what?”

“Wait a minute...” Clancy pointed through the window at the body. “There's no bullet hole.”

Thunder rumbled in the sky overhead. Dana turned to look where Clancy was looking and saw the skull. Its face was turned in their direction. The smooth red mask grinned, untroubled by cracks or puncture marks.

“What does that mean?” said Dana.

Clancy leaned forward, closer to the glass, narrowing his eyes. “It means... it isn't him. It's not Buckshaw. Oh God... *I know who that is!*”

In the very moment he said it... the skeleton sat up.

Dana shrieked, but didn't leap back. She couldn't look away. The skeleton raised an arm up over its head and turned its face to the sky, letting rivulets of acid cascade between its fingers and down over its polished cheeks. It opened its mouth and unfurled a long, black tongue to catch and taste the raindrops.

Dana tried to speak Clancy's name, but in her horror could make only a choking gasp. She watched as the skeleton turned its face towards her, as a glowing red light flickered up from the depths of its eye sockets.

“C— Clancy...”

The skeleton stood, arched its back as though stretching, then bent to pick something up from the ground.

“It's Jericho,” Clancy wailed. “We're dead.”

Dana only realized the skeleton was holding a rock when he threw it at them. Clancy saw it too, and pushed her away from the window, but wasn't quick enough to save himself. The pane shattered, spraying him with broken glass. His left arm, thrown up to protect himself, erupted into smoke as it was splashed with acid. He screamed.

Dana scrambled to her feet, clasped his other hand and pulled him away, leading him quickly out of the room. She cast one glance towards the broken window as they ran... and saw a pair of scaring red eyes hovering over a wide red grin.

***

For Clancy, the pain was so intense he very nearly blacked out. Consciousness ebbed and flowed even as his feet kept moving, pulled hurriedly onward by Dana. When he finally got a grip on his senses he found himself slumped in the corner of a darkened room. All he could hear was the drumming of rain on the shutters.

“Dana?”

“Baby...” She was a small shape, slinking through the shadows. She crawled into his arms and grasped for the brass ring in his stomach. His tentacle responded feebly.

“Where are we?” he croaked. His nostrils were full of the stink of his own burnt shell, muscle and bone.

“Third floor, servant's bedroom,” she said. There hadn't been any servants employed at the property for years – Buckshaw had said they were too expensive, and there was no need with Dana in the house – but the bedroom had a solid door with a lock. Dana prayed that was enough to keep it out. Whatever *it* was.

"How'd you get me up two flights of stairs?" Clancy asked.

She made a noise somewhere between laughing and weeping. "It wasn't easy."

Clancy shifted over onto one side then brought up his right hand and snapped his fingers. Suddenly there was light and Dana saw he was holding his enamel cigarette lighter. He turned its flame towards his left arm and got his first good look at it. It looked like Swiss cheese. Every raindrop had left its mark, burning a hole clean through whatever he'd put in its way.

"I reckon I won't look too pretty after this," he said. "Boy, I feel like hell."

"Clancy... what *was* that thing?"

"Jericho," he stated, sadly. "Last of the Puppeteers."

"What's that?"

He sighed. "It's a special type of person with the ability to get into someone's skin and take them over. Real rare. I think there was only ever about twenty of 'em and every last one worked as assassins or double agents for the mobs. Right up until Eyes and Broken Glass had one of their 'rainy afternoon' truces and decided using Puppeteers just wasn't 'playing fair.' So in the spirit of fair play they both handed each other a list of names – all the Puppeteers on their payroll and who they were pretending to be – and agreed to rub the whole lot of 'em out."

"And they... failed?"

Clancy shook his head. "They got 'em all but one. The very worst one. Jericho. They've been hunting for him ever since, but... never could find him."

Dana swallowed. Her voice was a whisper. "When did all this happen?"

Clancy shrugged with his good shoulder. "Must've been... maybe... six years ago now."

"Then... all that time... he was...?"

Clancy nodded. "Yeah, probably."

Dana slumped, her shoulders shaking. "I think I'm going to be sick."

"I wouldn't blame you."

"But... if the mobs are after him... he'll run. He has to. He'll run, won't he?"

"He will," Clancy said. "But not before he kills us. We've seen him and he won't be able to stand for that."

"What can we do?"

"Kill him first. A few bullets in the head might be a start, with no fat man to hide behind this time, but I left the gun in the study. There a phone in here?"

"Yeah, over there." Dana pointed to a nightstand in the corner.

"Call the cops," said Clancy. "They won't like moving around in a storm like this, but if you tell 'em Jericho's in the house they might just make an exception. Just don't... say anything about Buckshaw. We can come up with a story later."

"Okay," she said, and started across the floor on her hands and knees, eager to do whatever he asked of her if it offered the chance of survival. She snatched the receiver and held it to her ear, then, panic spreading across her face, tapped her fingers on the hook switch. "I can't get an outside line," she hissed. "I think... He must've taken one of the connecting phones off the hook."

"*Dana?*" The voice on the other end of the line was not her husband's. It was high-pitched, nasally and sneering. Exactly what she'd expect from a walking skeleton. "*Is that you, Dana?*"

She gripped the receiver tightly with both hands, wide eyes looking to Clancy for instruction. “Yes... Yes, this is me.”

“*Do you know... who I am?*”

Clancy pushed himself up onto his feet and, staying crouched, moved towards the door. Utilizing his healthy arm he made a series of signals intended to read: *Keep him talking. I'm going to make a break for the gun.*

Dana nodded. “Yes, I know. Your name's Jericho.”

“*I'm impressed. Who told you that?*”

“Clancy.” She spoke his name as she watched him unlock the door and slip out into the corridor. “He told me all about you.”

“*Ah, Clancy... My dear friend. All those drinks we shared, all those dinners... I never pegged the two of you. How is good old Clancy?*”

“Unconscious,” she lied. “He's badly burned.”

“*Yes, the acid rain. I've heard it hurts. Never been a problem for me. Something of a lifesaver, if you want to know the truth. Puppeteers tend to die with their puppets. I'd have surely suffocated under all of Buckshaw's fat if you hadn't put me out in the rain.*”

“So... when you think about it... we saved your life?”

Jericho laughed. “*I suppose that's one way to look at it. I do like that. Humor in the face of adversity. Y'know Dana, it's a delight to finally speak to you like this. Six years sharing the same bed and we hardly know each other! You don't know the real me and I –* clearly *– don't know the real you. What say you tell me what phone you're on, I'll come to you and we'll talk this whole silly mess over, huh?*”

“If I tell you where we are... you'll murder us.”

There was a long pause. Finally he said: “*Well, let's face it, honey. It's no more than you both deserve.*”

She felt a coldness in her stomach. “Please...”

"*Don't beg.*"

"There's no need for this. All I wanted was my husband out of the way. I wanted a new life with the man I love and enough money to make it worth living. And I've got that. You can go find some other poor sucker to wear. I'm not going to tell anyone about you. I've got no need."

"*You won't get the chance. And don't pretend this isn't personal. You... Wait...*"

She heard his receiver clatter to the floor. Heard the sound of hurried footsteps receding. "Jericho," she said. "Jericho, wait, please..."

A gunshot echoed through the house.

Dana ran to the door and threw herself out into the hallway. The blast of two more shots sounded in her ears and she froze, poised at the top of the stairs. The noise had seemed even louder than when Clancy had pulled the trigger in Buckshaw's face. She wanted to dash downstairs and face whatever scene awaited her, whoever the victor, but she couldn't. Terror had a grip on her.

Feeling hot tears on her face, she wilted, sinking sadly to the floor. With trembling hands she covered her face and bowed her head to the carpet.

Overhead the clouds made cannon roars of their own, while rain pounded on the roof.

Dana stayed that way a long time, unable to move even when she heard the creak of footsteps on the stairs, slowly climbing towards her. Only when his shadow enveloped her and he breathed her name could she look up.

"Dana..."

Blinking through her tears she saw him – a black giant looming above her.

"Clancy!" She raised herself up and lunged into his arms, kissing his chest. "Clancy, thank God. I was so afraid. Oh thank God! Thank God!"

Her hand moved instinctively to the aperture in his abdomen, felt the cold air around it and reached inside. Her delicate fingers, longing to feel his twisting softness, instead touched the barrel of a semi-automatic pistol, gripped in a bony hand.

Dana blinked and caught the glint of bone through the acid holes in his arm. Looking up to his face, she saw a pair of eyes burning red and indifferent. He'd been hollowed out.

Her thoughts raced ahead of the moment, a whirlwind of emotions and images churning almost beyond comprehension. She grasped for a coherent notion and found herself hoping that he wouldn't throw her body into the rain after he killed her. Even in death she didn't want to be nothing. She opened her mouth to tell him so...

But then the gun barked.

And suddenly it didn't matter anymore...

The Corridors of Power

The King of Broken Glass was so-named because he lived his life in the basements, dungeons, sewers and tunnels of the Grudge. He ran his empire from a city beneath the city. His meeting rooms were littered with the detritus that rained down from overhead. When money and bullets were set aside – not that they ever were – he was richest in rats and shattered bottles. And since the rats already had a monarch of their own, he found himself crowned King of Broken Glass.

By all accounts, it was a moniker he rather enjoyed. He liked the way it sounded when spoken and the violent imagery it conjured. Certainly, it sounded a damn sight better than his counterpart's.

The King of Eyes rose to prominence long after Broken Glass. The alias was always designed as a rejoinder of sorts – either an insult or tribute – but in time the power behind it came to equal, and eventually eclipse, his own. 'Eyes' lived his life in airships and penthouse apartments. His business was conducted on the roofs of skyscrapers or staring out from wrought-iron balconies.

And while the King of Broken Glass ventured above ground once a month to personally oversee payment collections, the King of Eyes never *ever* came below the twentieth floor. In the months following Broken Glass' assassination, pundits would point to this as being the deciding factor that sealed his doom.

On the morning of the attack, Broken Glass' convoy hit the Garment District first, then doubled back and took Bedsore Boulevard. As they turned onto 25th Street they were pinned by articulated trucks to the front and rear. Then a team of foot-soldiers moved in, peppered the vehicles with bullets, sprayed the ground around and underneath with petroleum and set it alight. Those who survived being cooked in the flames were killed in the ensuing gun battle. It was, in short, a massacre.

Word of Broken Glass' assassination reached the staff of the Norrland News a short time before their offices were flooded with gun-wielding gangsters. As with other cities and states where two factions vied for control, Grudgehaven was a city of dualities. For every politician on the payroll of Broken Glass, there was one working for Eyes. Same with dirty cops, doctors, lawyers, union reps... even plumbers. In the case of newspapers, the Grudge of course had two. The Grudgehaven Gazette had for some time operated under the subtle influence of the King of Eyes. The Norrland News – regrettably for its staff – had spent the better part of two decades backing the wrong horse.

On learning of the convoy attack, the Norrland News staff had a brief window of opportunity in which to make good their escape. In hindsight, probably the most sensible thing they could have done was set a match to the building and flee. They didn't. They remained at their desks, certainly troubled by what the impact of Broken Glass' death would be, but probably not imagining that their own lives were at risk. At least, not until they were faced by a team of pinstriped bone-crushers with sub-machine guns.

The lead bone-crusher, an armor-plated behemoth with a diesel engine in his chest and flames tattooed on his face, introduced himself thusly: “Listen up, you sludge-monkeys! My name is Breaker and I work for the King of Eyes.”

Not one of the twenty-two people in the office said a word.

“That's right,” Breaker continued. “Me and my men have been sent here to close this place down and that's exactly what we're going to do. But first... I want to see the editor. Hubble Hughes. Right here, right now.”

All heads turned towards a small office, separated from the main room by a thin partition. After a moment, a tired stick figure etched in tin and black ink shuffled his way out. When he was close enough to Breaker to be in his shadow, he adjusted the glasses on his hook-like nose, gripped his suspenders and straightened up as best he could.

“I'm Hubble Hughes,” he said, a trace of pride still audible beneath the fear.

Breaker motioned to two of his lackeys, who lifted the small man off of his feet and bundled him out of the building. Before anyone could relax, Breaker said: “And I got one more name. Cynthia Kline.”

This time there were gasps as the assembly turned their phosphorescent eyes on a middle-aged woman in the corner. She was shaped like an old-fashioned jukebox and probably shared a few of the same parts, dressed in an expensive turquoise dress suit and tilted pillbox hat. She was sitting at a large, old typewriter, sharing a desk with a decorative tea set and a score of framed photographs, each showing her in the company of a famed artist, socialite or politician.

At the sound of her name she turned, peered over her ornately-framed spectacles and said: “Me?”

“If your name's Cynthia Kline then yes,” Breaker answered.

“My name is Cynthia Kline,” she said. “But, well... are you quite sure?”

Breaker cocked his machine-gun. “Lady, I take my orders personally from the King of Eyes. Face to face. And he was very clear. Now, all that's gonna happen is... you're gonna come with me and we're gonna take a little ride. Got it?”

Kline nodded. The clockwork spider dangling from her hat danced as she moved her head. “I think I have it, yes. Just... let me get my things.” She gathered her handbag from under the desk and her coat from the stand by the wall, then turned to face her colleagues.

“Well,” she said, her chin trembling. “I suppose this is goodbye for... for now. Goodbye Hodge, Campbell, Rosh, Gill, Nizzy, Oli, Stewart, Cal, Walker, Hilley, Cockers, Park...”

“I don't have all day,” Breaker barked.

“And all the rest,” Cynthia said. “Take care of yourselves.”

Breaker ushered her through the door and out to a waiting limousine.

“I've always hated limousines,” she sighed.

Breaker opened the door and waved for her to get in. "Count yourself lucky," he said. "You could've been riding in the trunk. Like your boss."

***

The car sped across Midtown into the heart of the Spires, then ducked down a ramp into an underground parking lot beneath the Geronimo Building. Cynthia Kline was then led from the car to a small room beside the elevator, where she sat and waited at gunpoint for the next hour.

"I have to ask," she said, when she could stand the silence no more. "Why the flames?"

"What?" Breaker muttered.

"The flames," she repeated, waving her hand at him. "On your face. The ones that make it look like someone should be riding you in a drag race."

Breaker fixed her with a look that said his patience was running out. "I like flames. So I asked for flames."

"You look like a circus clown," she told him. "Of all the things to have tattooed on yourself. On your own face! What must your mother think? Presuming you even *know* your own mother."

"You shouldn't talk about my Ma." There was no trace of humor to his voice.
She scoffed. "I rather doubt there's very much to say on the matter."

Breaker took a step closer. The painted flames on his cheeks and temples appeared to deepen in color. "Y'know, if I wanted to... I could pop your head like an infected kidney."

Cynthia rolled her eyes and opened her handbag. "You sound very insecure when you speak like that." She produced a black cigarette, clutched in an ivory holder. "Can I trouble you for a lighter? Or should I just hold it against your forehead?"

Breaker was raising his hand when the elevator bell sounded behind him and the doors slid open. He froze in position for a moment, then took a deep breath, calmed himself and motioned for Kline to get onto her feet.

“What now?” she said.

“You're to get in the elevator,” he told her, through gritted yellow teeth. “It'll take you all the way to the 88th floor. He'll be there to meet you.”

“The King of Eyes?”

“That's all I know,” he growled, leaning closer. “All I can hope is that *if* you come back down... it'll be in the garbage chute!”

***

The elevator doors slid open on a dimly lit marble room. Cynthia stayed where she was for a moment, hands on hips, cigarette holder clamped between her teeth, wondering just what in hell she was walking into. When she stepped out, the doors slid shut behind her.

There was nothing in the room. No people, no furniture, no windows, no signs. Nothing of interest except an etching of a giant eye staring out of the floor. Not subtle. In the wall opposite was an archway leading into a long, dark and narrow corridor. She crossed to it and stood on the threshold, trying to see what was at the other end. She could make out a glimmer of light, but nothing more substantial.

It was entirely probable, she surmised, that the smartest thing to do was stay where she was until someone came to her and told her to do otherwise. Unfortunately, she didn't have the patience for that. She checked her reflection in the polished marble, made sure her hat was at the correct angle, none of her makeup had smudged, then started down the corridor.

She moved quickly at first, then slowed when she realized how jagged and uneven the stonework around her was. The walls of the corridor appeared to have been sculpted out of some black rock with which she was unfamiliar. It was too dark to tell what any of the designs were supposed to be, but at various points the cut rock jutted out into her path, making it difficult to navigate with any speed.

She managed till she was almost halfway, when her sleeve snagged and tore on one of the exposed edges. “Damn,” she muttered.

“Damn...” a voice echoed, not her own. “Damn.”

“Daaaaamn”

“Damned, damned...”

The voices came from all around her. Male, haunted, desperate. She kept moving.

“Damn you...”

“Damn.”

“Damn it all...”

“Damn him. Damn his eyes.”

“Damn... damn...”

Her eyes caught shivers of movement in the walls. The sculptures shifted, slowly twisting, bending their forms towards her. Just a few steps from the light, a black, bulbous shape leaned out in front of her, slick with a glistening silver fluid. As she neared it, a pair of holes sprung open in its smooth surface and were lit with a pale green glow. She halted, realizing in horror that she was staring into a pair of eyes.

As she looked on, stricken with fear, a thin wound appeared beneath the eyes and split open, revealing a slack, drooling mouth. “Daaaaaamn,” it moaned. “Daaammm... the paaaaiiiinnn....”

She smacked it in the face with her handbag and ran, quick as she could, into the light.

“Pain! The paaaaiiin!” Hands reached out for her. “SUFFERING!” Claws scratched at her clothing. “Annnnggguiissh!” Knots of stretched limbs rubbed against her legs, trying to trip her up.

She stumbled and fell, screaming, into the arms of tall, broad-shouldered man in a double-breasted suit. “Relax,” he told her. “They can't hurt you.”

Cynthia blinked and looked about her, realizing she was on the other side of the corridor in a white-tiled office. The creatures in the darkness behind her writhed in torment. She gazed up at the man into whose chest she'd thrown herself. He was more than a foot taller than her, with a smooth domed head and red fiberglass goatee. She saw her own terrified face reflected in his mirrored spectacles.

“You must be Cynthia Kline,” he boomed, in a deep baritone. “My name is Horace Wexford. But you probably know me as the King of Eyes.”

***

He poured tea while the monstrosities in the corridor settled down and went back to playing dead. Cynthia took a seat opposite a vast, polished white desk on which sat nothing at all. Not one piece of stationary, not one scrap of paper. The chair was too high for her and her feet dangled an inch or so above the floor, but she made up her mind not to complain.

“Your jacket's torn,” he said as he passed her a cup and saucer. “I'll pay for a replacement.”

Her hands were shaking as she reached for the tea. “It's no worry. I was getting tired of it anyway.”

He smiled. “You needn't be afraid of me, Ms Kline. I'm rather a fan of yours.”

She wondered if this was an ironic preamble to murder. “Really? You read my column?”

Wexford sat down behind the mighty desk. He was so big even it failed to dwarf him. “Every one. It helps to leaven my mood after reading the poisonous fictions littering the rest of your regrettable periodical.”

Cynthia bowed her head into her tea. “I wouldn't know about that.”

“No.” Wexford grinned. “You've never penned a word about me. You'd rather wax about that charmed constellation of odious imbeciles masquerading as the *great and good*.”

"I *am* a gossip columnist, Mr Wexford. Writing about celebrities is what I'm paid for."

"And very good you are, too. You have a vicious way with a turn of phrase, Ms. Kline. Clean, cutting... witty. I admire all that. And I would like to offer you a position."

"A position?" Cynthia sipped nervously at her tea. It was much too hot and burned her mouth, but she tried not let it show.

"Nothing unsavory," said Wexford. "And believe me, you're in need of the work. Your office is burning to the ground as we speak."

Cynthia gasped.

Wexford displayed another in his repertoire of reassuring smiles. "Please don't worry. No one will have been inside. The Grudge has one King now and needs only one newspaper. I'll be amalgamating both staffs under the banner of the Grudgehaven Gazette. I don't blame your colleagues for the appalling things they've written about me over the years. They were working under the direction of my enemies, after all. Those that are worth keeping will be kept on. Those that are not will be allowed to go on their way, off to find *real* work of some description. None will be harmed. Excusing your editor, of course." The smile dropped from his face for a moment, leaving a hard gaze, rich in hate. "I'm afraid he simply took rather too much *relish* in his work."

Cynthia was too frightened to ask what he meant by that, so instead asked: "What's the job?"

The smile returned. "I want you to be my personal biographer."

She raised an eyebrow. "You're kidding."

He leaned forward, placing his hands together on the desk and interlocking his fingers. "Ms. Kline, this is a wonderful day for me. My only rival has been vanquished. His heirs are dead. His assets are in the process of being assumed into my own empire. When that process is complete... I will *own* the Grudge. I am – and I say this will all humility – the most important man ever to have lived in this city in its history, yet the people do not even know my name. Doesn't that sound like a situation that needs to be corrected? And don't my exploits sound like the makings of a tome you would want to read?"

"Surely," she answered, speaking honestly. "But why me?"

"Because I like the way you write, Ms. Kline. I think you might be the only scribe in this city capable of doing justice to the subject." The ringer of a telephone sounded. Wexford made an apologetic face and reached under the desk. His hand returned holding a thin white receiver. "Yes?"

Cynthia heard a woman's voice on the other end of the line.

"Really?" he said. "At this time? ... No, no, I'm sure that will be fine. ... All right, come on up." He hung up the phone, stood and smiled again at Cynthia. "My daughter needs to speak with me. I'm sure it's not urgent, but you know what young women are like."

"Oh yes," Cynthia said, rising onto her feet. "Yes, of course."

"We'll talk more about this tomorrow," he said. "I'll send a car to collect you at noon. Breaker or someone will drive you home. And don't think I've forgotten about the jacket. Expect payment."

"Um..." Cythia pointed down the corridor. "Is that the only way out?"

"Ah. Yes. I'm afraid so, but as I said, you needn't worry. It's more for decoration than anything else. They might complain a bit, but they can't harm you."

Resigning herself to the fact she had no other choice, Cynthia gripped her handbag in front of her and started back along the corridor, moving as quickly and as quietly as she could. Though she kept her mouth shut, she could sense the walls were aware of her presence.

Halfway along, the sequence began again. "Siiiiiiin..." one of them whispered.

"Sin," another answered.

"Siiin... SIN!"

Fixing her gaze on the marble room ahead, she broke into a run, desperate to be free.

“Sin!” they cried “SIN! SIN!”

A hand clutched at her arm and pulled her about. She recognized the distorted, grime-smeared face that bubbled out of the wall before it spoke. Broken spectacles dangling from lopsided ears, hook nose dripping with silver, he dropped his jaw and wailed: “CYNTHIA!”

It was Hubble Hughes. Her editor.

***

“Drop me off on the corner,” she told Breaker.

“I was told to take you all the way home,” he replied from the driver's seat. “Right to the door.”

She sighed and pinched the bridge of her nose with her fingertips. “It's only a few doors away and I want to buy a bottle of gin. After the day I've had I don't think that's too extravagant a request.”

He stopped the limo by the drug store on the corner of 19th and Hekkate, allowed her just enough time to get both feet out the door and then took off, his tail-lights a receding red blur in the darkness. Cynthia bought a quart of gin and a cigarette lighter from the charming plastic man behind the counter, then stepped back out onto the street. She was on the sidewalk no more than a couple of seconds before a battered blue Studebaker sedan pulled up beside her.

The passenger door popped open and the driver flashed a badge. “Get in.”

She groaned. “Really?”

“Now,” he answered.

With the greatest of reluctance she slid in beside him and pulled the door shut. Then they were cutting back into traffic and speeding north again.

“Name's Lieutenant Drake Parker. Grudgehaven Police Department,” he said.

“I can't imagine why you'd think I'd care.”

“I'm part of a task force assigned to gather evidence against the King of Eyes.” He was a wiry man, almost skeletal in form, with not a trace of bulk to fill out the brown leather trench-coat he wore. His rectangular head was flecked with rust, eyes dark and tired.

“I thought the King of Eyes *owned* the police force,” said Cynthia.

“Not all of it. Not yet. He has a lot of influence, which explains why we haven't had much success so far... but I'm hoping to change that.”

“Not with my help.”

He pulled hard on the wheel and the car swung left into an alleyway. He checked the rear, then cut the engine. “Just hear me out.”

“It doesn't look like I've any choice.” She went into her bag for a cigarette. “Go on.”

He turned towards her, revealing a long, deep scar down the left side of his face. It looked to have been repaired with iron staples and a soldering gun. “If I'm on the money here,” he said, “you just took the job of writing up his life story.”

Cynthia had the cigarette holder back between her teeth. When she spoke it was out one side of her mouth. “You are a clever boy, aren't you? What's it to you?”

“It's a very privileged position. There isn't a lot he can tell you about himself that wouldn't implicate him in a dozen rackets, a hundred money laundering operations or close to a thousand murders.”

Her lighter snapped shut as she exhaled a cloud of smoke. “We haven't discussed the details yet,” she said. “But I imagine he'll want the book published posthumously. For posterity's sake. That or it will be very heavily edited. Nothing litigious.”

Parker shook his head. “No. He's not the kind to plan for his own death. Thinks he'll live forever. And by the time the book's ready for publication he expects to have the whole city in his pocket. He'll be invincible. You won't have to edit a word. We're dealing with the King of *Egos* here.”

“You think he's wrong about that?”

“I'm scared he might be right. That's why I can't afford to let you go back to him... without a wire.”

She laughed, once, more in outrage than humor. “You're not serious. You expect me to go willingly into the lion's den with a tape recorder slung over my shoulder and a microphone up my sleeve? No thank you!”

“Nothing so obvious. They can do wonderful things these days. You could be wearing it in plain sight and he'd never know.” He reached out and pinched the clockwork spider hanging from her hat. It squirmed at his touch. “This, maybe. Where did you get it?”

She waved his hand away. “Klonmeyer on 9th. And I'm not helping you.”

“You might think twice if you knew what he was capable of.”

“I know *exactly* what he's capable of. I've seen it. He doesn't just kill people, you know. He... Wait a moment...” Her brow furrowed. “This is a test, isn't it?”

“What?”

She pointed the hot end of the cigarette at him. “You're one of his. He sent you to try to trick me into betraying him. That's a lousy thing to do.”

He held out his hands. “I swear. I'm on the level.”

She gave him a brief glance up and down, then turned about so she was staring out the window. “Take me home, Lieutenant Parker. This conversation's over.”

He leaned forward, opening his mouth like he was about to try another angle, then thought better of it and shut up. With an almost pantomime level of reluctance he turned back to the wheel and started the engine up.

"The Grudge can't tolerate a kingpin, Ms. Kline," he said, when they were moving again. "The city will rise against him or collapse beneath him. Sooner or later you'll have to choose where to stand."

***

When at last she made it into her apartment she found two boxes waiting for her in the hall. They were filled with personal items from her desk at work. Every one smelled faintly of paraffin.

Cynthia poured herself a gin, but it didn't relax her as much as she hoped it might and she stopped after the first glass. Unable to eat, not wanting to think, she popped a couple of pills, undressed and went to bed.

She spent the night fitfully waking, constantly afraid the walls were coming to get her.

Breaker was outside her door at noon the next day, just as Wexford had promised. This time they drove to the Sunquist Building, where Cynthia enjoyed a long lunch with her subject in the penthouse, with no melting horrors to trouble her.

She took many notes and in her head began to devise an outline for the proposed manuscript.

***

It continued that way for weeks. Cynthia spent a couple of hours with the King of Eyes each day, enjoying the finest foods and beverages the Grudge had to offer, while he regaled her with tall tales of his early life and career. He was charming, erudite and always careful to skip past the gorier details, remarking: "But we'll get into that on another occasion..."

Cynthia found herself slipping quite easily into the rhythm of the thing. She felt no pressure. The hours were good, their conversations enjoyable, her subject legitimately fascinating. At the end of each session she spent an hour or so writing in whatever office space they provided her, then was escorted home, free to enjoy the rest of her day.

The pay was more than fair. On the clear understanding she was to discuss her work with no one, she resumed her calendar of social engagements and only in the briefest moments – whenever she imagined she saw a battered blue Studebaker disappearing round the nearest corner – did she feel a twinge of discomfort.

At no point during this period was she forced to endure the gauntlet of grasping hands and snapping jaws on the 88th floor of the Geronimo Building. Wexford met her in different buildings all over the city, but never there. She began to wonder if that first meeting had all been part of some test of her character. She still wondered the same thing about Parker.

Such notions were challenged the day Breaker drove her back to the Geronimo Building and directed her to the elevator. Again, she found herself in the marble room, faced with a corridor of squirming torment. Again they called for her, reached out to her, damn near captured her. Again, she emerged at a run and fell, gasping, into Wexford's arms.

His tiled office was red. The walls, ceiling, floor, even the huge desk, stacked high with papers.

"Do you like it?" He grinned. "I had it redecorated."

***

She did her best to take notes during his monologues, but couldn't keep her hands from shaking. Dressed in a pressed white shirt and golden waistcoat, white trilby casually tossed onto the desk, he paced back and forth in front of the red stained glass window, vibrantly recounting his battles with old foes. After forty minutes or so, she could stand no more.

"Can I ask..." she said, interrupting. "Can I ask a question?"

His hands, which had been in the process of making some sweeping gesture, froze in mid-air. He looked to her over his forearm, his lips slowly curling upwards. "Of course you can."

She pointed her pen at the shadowed passage of frozen nightmares behind her. "What is that?"

"That?" His eyes darted to the corridor, plated eyebrows sneaking upwards, as though he was seeing it for the first time. "Oh, *that*. I told you before. It's nothing, really. Decorative more than anything else. But we can get into the details on another occasion..."

"No," she stated, as simply and forcefully as she possibly could. "That's not good enough. I take it we'll be having more meetings in this office?"

"Yes," he replied, as he eased into his chair. "This is *my* office. It's where I conduct most of my business. I've only been taking meetings elsewhere these last weeks because of the makeover."

"Right. Well I'm not doing it again. I'm not coming back through here till I know what that damn thing is. It's about time you started treating me with some respect and told me plainly what the hell it is you do to people. No more sugar-coated half truths. You have to speak openly and honestly with me or this book won't be worth spit. Do you understand?"

He stared at her, grimly. "Yes. I understand." He reached across the desk to the pot of tea that had been stewing while they talked and poured himself a cup. Without looking up he said: "The corridor is a preserver, of sorts. Both walls are fashioned from Leeching rock, a kind of geological anomaly prevalent in the Blacklands region south of the Dam. There's a sculptor in town who does a lot of work with it. He calls it a 'confused mineral,' since it can't seem to decide what it is. At room temperature it wavers between solid and molten form. Come into direct contact with it and it will paralyze you and feed on you. There's not a lot to eat in the Blacklands, so the Leeching rock tends to tease out its meals, sometimes for centuries. It drains the body first, then the mind and finally the soul." He sipped at the tea and licked his lips. "The corridor – my own design, incidentally – is effectively a private prison."

"And a form of execution," Cynthia said, her voice a tremulous whisper.

"Eventually." Wexford nodded. His expression darkened. "It's also a torture device, if you want to know the whole truth. You said you did. The Leech can be excruciatingly painful when feeding. At other times it smothers and preserves its meal. Makes for a very slow, very unpleasant death."

"Why?" The face of Hubble Hughes flickered in her vision. "Why not just kill them?"

He considered the question for a moment. "I've killed many people, Ms. Kline. A great many. It causes me no guilt and hardly any effort. It's a punishment meted out to the unremarkable in times of disappointment. A real threat – a genuine troublemaker – deserves far worse than that. Those that have tried to outwit me, outflank me, *destroy* me... they deserve to suffer. And when they're lucid, some of them are able to offer counsel. Who better to consult on a stratagem than a viable – albeit vanquished – opponent? They'll happily divulge the best their calculating minds can provide in return for a little pain relief. Every devious brain added to that corridor strengthens my own position. It's made me the man I am today. Plus, as I said... the decorative element."

Cynthia felt queasy. She couldn't help but be sickened by the specimen seated opposite her. Yet she tried her hardest not to show it.

"The King of Broken Glass then," she said. "Your greatest enemy of all. I take it he's there."

Wexford stiffened at the name. "No. He's... dead. Quite dead."

Cynthia's eyes narrowed as the clockwork spider hanging from her hat contracted its legs into its body. "You have proof of that?"

He grinned at her. It was a sudden and grotesque sight. "Whatever for? He's dead!"

The phone rang, cutting her off on the verge of another question. Wexford picked it up, spoke a few words into the mouthpiece, then hung up.

He glanced to Cynthia, apparently considering her worth for a moment, then stood, buttoned his waistcoat and snatched up the trilby. "I have urgent business to attend to. You should come along. Might make for a diverting anecdote."

She hardly felt in a position to refuse.

***

The airship crept across the skyline like a poisonous cloud. It rose away from the Spires and struck out into the night, heading east over the reservoir. Cynthia and Wexford stood in the gondola, staring out across the black waters, not speaking. He was drinking champagne and said it was the only thing he allowed anyone to drink on all nine of the vessels in his floating fleet. He had offered Cynthia a glass, but she'd declined, saying the ship's movements made her stomach ache. The symptoms of which she complained were truthful enough. The cause was not.

They were joined on the deck by a small crew manning the controls and a single armed guard. When they were a few miles out over the reservoir, Wexford signaled to the guard, who slid open the door to a separate, smaller room, and ushered a pair of men through.

The first was a stranger to Cynthia, but he looked much like any of the King of Eyes' goons – a slick carbuncle of engine parts, thrown into a black suit and hosed down with aftershave. The second, smaller man, hobbled tiredly behind, dressed in creased corduroys and a stained shirt.

She recognized him as Jed Regan, head of the ChaBro Workers Union.

"Champagne, Fox?" Wexford asked, holding out the bottle.

"Thanks, boss," said the black suit, restlessly fidgeting with the rings on his fingers.

Wexford poured the goon a glass and turned the bottle towards Regan, who shook his head.

"Oh come on, Regan," Wexford said. "This pious, impoverished act of yours grows tiresome. Indulge yourself."

"No thank you," Regan answered. His voice was lacking its usual brimstone. "I'd rather we just made this as quick as possible. Whatever it is."

"Very well," Wexford said. "It's the big vote at the end of the month. I want your assurance that you will tell your men not to strike. You will tell them to take the new deal."

Regan laughed weakly. "You mean the new deal that'll leave my men working twice as hard and put all the reward in your pocket? That deal?"

Wexford smiled. He turned towards Cynthia, checking that she was carefully observing the conversation, then looked back to Regan. "That's the one, yes. If you'd be so kind."

"I can't believe you brought me all the way out here for this. In a God-damned blimp!" Regan raised a thick copper finger towards Fox. "That's the same deal this knucklehead's been trying to sucker me into for a year now. What makes you think *you* can convince me?"

Wexford shrugged. "That's a good question. Maybe... this?" He drew a pistol from behind his back, raised his arm and pulled the trigger.

Cynthia threw her hands over her mouth to stifle a scream as Fox's head burst apart in a flurry of grease and shrapnel. Still clutching his champagne glass, he dropped to his knees and crashed forward onto the metal floor.

Wexford turned the gun towards his face and blew smoke away from the barrel. "I gave him a very simple task," he said. "That's what he gets for disappointing me. Can you imagine, Regan, what I might do were *you* to disappoint me?"

Cynthia could imagine.

Regan's pale eyes were on Fox's corpse, staring at the pool of bubbling oil under his shattered face as it spread outwards.

"I'm not afraid of you," he whispered, barely audible above the thrum of the ship's engines. "I'm not afraid of death."

"No, of course not," Wexford said as he stepped forward, bridging the gap between them. "You're an old man. Clearly a seriously *unwell* man. I'd wager you'll be dead soon enough without any assistance from me. But, you see, were you to disappoint me, I wouldn't kill you. No. I'd start with your men. Maybe a few would go missing here and there, no one would know what had become of them... except for you. You'd know. And if that didn't convince you I'd have to start on their wives, their children... Eventually, presuming you're as stubborn as you claim, I'd work my way up to *your* wife, *your* children. I'll make it so that you have nothing left to fight *for.* And what then? You can't beat me. There's not a soul in the Grudge capable of denying me what I'm owed. So, speaking as a King unto his subject, I implore you... *capitulate*."

***

Fox's body was thrown out of a hatch somewhere over the reservoir before they turned and sailed with the wind, back into the city. Cynthia didn't see what they did with Regan. He was taken to another part of the ship and was still on board, as far as she knew, when she and Wexford disembarked on the roof of the Geronimo Building.

One of Wexford's assistants was waiting for him. "Your daughter wishes to speak with you, sir," he said. "She's in the polo lounge."

Cynthia didn't know what the hell a "polo lounge" was, but reckoned it was probably even worse than she could imagine.

"Thank you," Wexford said, as he turned to his biographer. "I'll have to go to her. She's going through an especially challenging time. You can find your way down, yes?"

"It's true what they say about you," Cynthia said. They were the first words she had spoken to him in over an hour. "You won't be satisfied till you have the whole city in your pocket."

Wexford frowned, looked quickly about to check that none of his men were listening, then took off his hat and leaned in towards her, smiling like a spurned lover in anticipation of a kiss. "*Who* says that?"

Cynthia made no reply. For what felt like the longest time they stood there, staring at one another in silence, nothing passing between them but the wind.

Finally, he said: "I will be happy, Ms. Kline, when everyone has learned to pay their dues. Till then... needs must." He sniffed and straightened. "You know, I'm glad we had that little talk earlier, the one about honesty. It's important that we can trust one another, and be truthful about who we are. I think... I think this could be the start of something *truly extraordinary*."

***

Before they were halfway to her street she told Breaker to drop her off at the corner store.

“More gin?” he sneered.

She didn't answer him, but when they reached Hekkate he did as she'd asked.

She didn't go into the store. She stood on the corner and waited. Waited damn near twenty minutes before the blue Studebaker pulled lazily up to the curb.

A few minutes later the two of them were sitting in the same alley as before.

“Y'know, for an overworked cop, you don't seem to spend much time at the office,” she said. “Or on cases. Or anywhere that isn't in this car, following me around.”

Parker sighed. “If this is about you not trusting me...”

“I don't,” she snapped. “I think I've made that quite clear. And you've done nothing to convince me you're on the level.”

“Yeah...” He rubbed his iron-stubbled chin. “Well... I had an idea about that. In the meantime...” He went into his pocket and produced a clockwork spider on a golden thread. It was a perfect match for the one she wore. He held it out to her. “All you do is give it a little squeeze till you hear a click,” he said. “It can record up to forty hours. If we can't catch him incriminating himself in that time, we won't catch him at all.”

“He has to be stopped,” Cynthia said. She caressed the spider in her palm. It fidgeted at her touch. “I'm certain of that much at least.”

“Well when you've got what you need all you do is box it up and send it to D.A. Willem Xenod.”

“Not you?”

He shook his head. “Not me. But Willem's one of the few. He won't let you down.”

She cringed. "I'm not saying I'll go through with it. I'm not saying that. No guarantees."

"Never." He spoke from a place of understanding. "Not in this town."

***

She stood a long time in front of the mirror the next morning. She hadn't invested so much time in the study of her own reflection since her teen years – and, it had to be said, she looked much better now. Her previous book – published two decades before her current project – had been a how-to guide for Grudgehaven girls, packed full of makeup tips; ways to trick the male population into thinking you weren't quite as hideous as they were. Every copy sold had come with a free trowel, courtesy of her sponsors at Chemlik, to assist with the layering on of grease and powder by the solid ounce.

Today it wasn't her makeup that concerned her so much as the accessories. She held both spiders up to her hat, side by side, comparing one against the other. *If I didn't know,* she wondered, *could I tell the difference?*

Down on the street a car honked its horn – Breaker announcing his arrival. The interruption forced her to make a decision. Her own clockwork companion curled into a displeased ball as she tucked him back in the jewelry drawer and pinned Parker's arachnid spy to her head.

***

For once it wasn't the corridor that frightened her. She stood trembling in the marble room, far more terrified of who or what awaited her on the other side. More than once her hand, moving almost independently of her mind, went for the spider, almost ripping it away, crushing it and throwing it into the bottom of her bag. She managed to get control of herself, but it was a close-run thing. In her life, she'd never cared greatly for heroes, equating bravery with stupidity. On the verge of double-crossing the King of Eyes, she certainly didn't feel brave. She felt stupid.

Wexford's enemies ignored her as she passed. They were black statues, frozen in expressions of dread and sorrow. She tried not to look at their faces, but found it all too easy to imagine herself among them, writhing in futile fits, her body and mind being bled away, till nothing remained but torment. For a moment she saw her own face there, weeping silver tears in the shadows.

She made up her mind then, just a few steps from the office. *I can't do this. There's no way.* She grabbed the spider, felt it writhe in her palm, and made to tear it out. A black claw reached out from the wall, wrapped around her wrist and held it where it was.

She shrieked and turned to face her distorted attacker as he melted out of the shadows.

“Pleeeeasssse... Doooooon't...” His clouded eyes looked like lumpen milk and his face looked like it had been scorched black. She recognized him by the scar, mended with iron staples and a soldering gun. “Pleeeeaaaseee...”

“You've met Lieutenant Parker then, I see.” It was only when he spoke that Cynthia realized Wexford was standing beside her. He reached over and brushed the detective's hand away like it was a dead branch, then put his arm around Cynthia and led her through to the office. “The latest edition,” he said, as he guided her into her chair. “We've been searching for him for a long time. Didn't think we would ever find him, but he finally slipped up last night. Some of the boys brought him in after midnight. They call it luck, but I wouldn't call it that. It's more... there's a word for it. A phrase... It'll come to me.”

Cynthia's hands were trembling. She tried to hide it by gripping the arms of her chair. “Why...?” So choked up she could hardly speak. “Why him?”

Wexford waved his hand dismissively. “Oh, he was part of some special team the police put together years ago, back before the Commissioner and I became so close. He was a little too enthusiastic, a little too good at his job... eventually I was forced to deal with him.” He reached across his desk for the tea-pot and poured them both a cup. “Unfortunately, while the bomb meant for him succeeded in killing his family, he escaped relatively unscathed. Turned vigilante, and he's been a thorn in my side ever since. It's quite a relief to finally have him.”

“You mean...” she said. “He could have really hurt you.”

He considered the question a moment, then nodded. “Yes. He was one of the few. Even fewer now.” He smiled and picked up his cup, then turned to the window and stared out across his city. “You see it's all falling into place, now. Every little piece. The city bends its will to me...” He snapped his fingers. “That's it. That's good. You should write it down.”

“I will.” Her hand went into her bag, taking out a notepad and pen. “Please continue.” She stole a single, quick glance back at the corridor. *Congratulations, Lt. Parker,* she thought. *You finally convinced me.*

As Wexford launched into his latest soliloquy, she turned to a fresh page and positioned the pen over the paper. Then, as casually as she could, she reached with her free hand for the spider, pinched it between thumb and forefinger, and squeezed till she heard a *click.*

A Real Piece of Work

Alesa's mother's body began to rot three weeks before she died. In her final days, the old woman – once so loving and so beloved – was reduced to a moaning mound of suppurating wax, skin and bone. Poor Alesa, who along with her girth and lumpy, unpleasant features had inherited her mother's sense of compassion, was left alone to care for her as best she could.

She mopped her brow with white vinegar, lanced her boils twice a day and did her best to ensure their small house south of the Norrland Dam stayed warm, all round the clock. She did everything the local healer had advised, even reading to her for a couple of hours each night, as a way of putting her to sleep. The stench from her mother's body was worst in the evenings, but Alesa endured it in the hopes she was offering some comfort. The only book in the house was the Savior's Bible – of which there were several thousand copies – and Alesa worried her mother might find the content upsetting. However, the healer assured her that her mother was far beyond comprehending the meaning of the words. It was the soothing sound of her daughter's voice that mattered.

When her mother entered the final stage of the disease – a place beyond comfort, where even breathing caused her immeasurable pain – Alesa went back to the healer and begged for a sprig of Locust's Kiss. This she mashed into a paste with sour milk and rubbed on her mother's lips. In just a few moments the old woman was finally at peace. Alesa then placed coins over her eyes and wrapped her in bedsheets, before dragging her out to the walled dirt yard at the rear of the house. She dug a hole with a shovel borrowed from a neighbor, then rolled the body in and covered it with mud. She made offerings of silk, tin, bread and tobacco for the Widow, Warrior, Traveler and Guardian, then fashioned a cross from a pair of sticks. This was the Savior's symbol and she planted it in the ground a few inches from where her mother's head was buried. When all this was done, Alesa knelt at her mother's graveside, said a brief prayer and began to weep.

It was at this moment her father, absent from the family home for the last two months, chose to make his return.

“Hush child.” His cold hand gripped her shoulder like a hawk's talon. Even on her knees, turned away from him, she could smell the liquor on his clothes and breath. “You mustn't be afraid,” he slurred. “Trust in the Savior and all will be well. Now come inside and pack your things.”

***

Alesa had no say in the matter. Though she was almost seventeen and had single-handedly nursed her mother through the final stages of a bitter, brutal disease, she was, in the thick-veined eyes of her father, a mere child, ignorant of the ways of the world. Though he had spent more time these last years in the bottom of a bottle than in consultation with the scriptures, he took his wife's death as a sign from God that it was time to move on. There was work to be done in the Grudge.

Alesa would be the first to admit she knew little about the world beyond the end of her street. Caring for her mother had left her little time for exploration in her young life and she had a natural inclination to hide herself away, so aware was she of her own ugliness and deformities. Even among the malformations of the Damned, she was shunned. However, as naïve as she was, even she recognized that religion had become an outmoded concept in the Grudge and the city was no place for missionaries.

“Which is exactly why we *must* go,” her father told her. “It is our duty to seek out the wretched and the rotten and confront them with the Savior's love. And I cannot imagine a place more wretched or rotten that Grudgehaven.”

He sold their home and belongings and bought an exhausted jalopy, held together with string and sealing wax. When they'd passed the Norrland Dam and arrived in the heart of Downtown, he sold the car too and used the cash to book a month's stay in a crumbling hotel on Chancroid.

She spent the night in a filthy room not much bigger than the hole in which she'd laid her mother. Though it was cramped, humid and reeked of old blood and sweat, she was, for the moment, counting her blessings.

She was thankful that her father had not had them sharing a room, as the hotelier had lasciviously suggested when the preacher originally baulked at the cost of two.

It was difficult to settle with all the noise filtering through the walls – plumbing, loud conversations, recorded swing music, snoring, the rutting of anonymous couples. Eventually, however, sleep came. She drifted away and into the same dreams of pain and degradation that plagued her most nights.

When she awoke it was to darkness and the muted sound of her father's prayers through the wall.

***

"*But mark this! There will be terrible times in the last days. People will be lovers of themselves, lovers of money, boastful, proud, abusive, disobedient to their parents, ungrateful, unholy, without love, unforgiving, slanderous, without self-control, brutal, not lovers of the good, treacherous, rash, conceited, lovers of pleasure rather than lovers of God – having a form of godliness but denying its power. Have nothing to do with them!*"

Alesa's father's words blared from audio speakers strapped to her arms as she wandered through the crowd. LED displays pinned to her chest and back read: TIMOTHY 3:1-5. At her waist was an open cloth bag loaded to the brim with miniature Bibles no larger than a cigarette lighter. She gathered up fistfuls and held them out to passers-by, who dutifully ignored her and went about their own business. The boardwalk was crowded with merchants, tourists and vendors of every shape, age and sex. They fought their way through the crowds, pushing against the tide. Faces flashed past Alesa. Ugly, scarred, sneering. Every last one terrified her.

"*People who want to get rich fall into temptation and a trap and into many foolish and harmful desires that plunge men into ruin and destruction,*" her father bellowed from somewhere across the bustling market. "*For the love of money is a root of all kinds of evil*!"

The displays on her chest and back blinked: TIMOTHY 6:9-10.

“How you doing, Timothy?” A fish-faced dwarf in tortoise-shell sunglasses grinned up at her.

“Yeah, hi,” laughed his companion. “Nice to meet you, Tim!” They each snatched a handful of Bibles out of her bag and pelted her with them as she turned and ran.

“Where you goin,’ Tim?” The dwarf laughed. “Just trying to be friendly!”

It was three days since their arrival in the heart of the city and the third straight day of her father’s preaching in the 32nd Street Market. Alesa was beginning to get used to the taunts and attacks. This was to be her life now. She took no pleasure in it.

She darted through the crowd on bare feet at the ends of fat, stubby legs. A few laughed or snorted when they caught sight of her, but most failed to register her existence. She reached the corner of the squarc and broke free from the horde of monstrous bodies, then sank down onto an unoccupied step to catch her breath.

“*There are six things the SAVIOR hates,*” Alesa’s father continued, through the crackling loudspeakers. “*Seven that are detestable to him: haughty eyes, a lying tongue, hands that shed innocent blood, a heart that devises wicked schemes, feet that are quick to rush into evil, a false witness who pours out lies and a man who stirs up dissension among brothers…*”

How she wished she could shut him up.

“Hey you! Proverb! Whatever your name is!” Alesa looked around to find a woman addressing her; tall, athletic and molded from polished silver. Alesa regarded her like a mythical creature come to life. A mane of dark red hair, delicately braided. Eyes of red, flecked with gold and plump, smiling lips. She wore a single garment – a white tunic of sheer fabric that clung to her sculpted curves, stretching tight over large, round breasts and ending a fifth of the way down her thigh. “Can’t you keep it down, huh?” she called. “I don’t want that trash talk interfering with my business!”

The woman stood at the top of the wrought-iron staircase on which Alesa was seated, at the entrance to the Weeping Worm saloon. She was a better advertisement for the business than any of the frayed posters for “FINE WINES,” “CARD GAMES” and “DANCING GIRLS” plastered around the door.

“I can't, okay?” Alesa yelled, suddenly finding her voice as tears filled her eyes. “I don't know how!”

“What?” the woman called back. It was hard to hear above the constant drone of her father.

Alesa was about to shout again when she felt a rough hand clamp down on her knee and heard an old man hiss: “Well lookee at this...”

She spun round to find a gray half-man leering up at her. His body stopped at the waist, molded into a caterpillar track, and he crawled with his hands as he thrust his head between her legs. “You're one o' them *Old Town* gals...” His toothless mouth spilled drool as neared her skin.

Alesa screamed in the same moment a hard kick from the toe-end of a stiletto sent the old man tumbling backwards. He landed face-down on the cobbles, dark blood leaking slowly from a cut in his temple.

“Y'oughta learn some manners, Murphy!” the silver woman shouted as she checked her shoe for damage. “Maybe that'll remind you.” She turned to Alesa, who huddled pale and frightened beside her on the steps. “Lost his legs in a crash a few years back,” she explained. “Along with half his brain. And his balls. Not that it seems to have slowed him down. You all right?”

“*We are forever tested by temptation. Our weaknesses, in pursuit, are like wild hounds, tracking us to wherever we may hide...*”

“What?” Alesa said.

The woman made the latest in a series of irritated faces, reached down, and tugged a wire free from the apparatus around Alesa's neck. Her father's voice suddenly sputtered and died. Alesa, blinking away tears, felt an unbearable surge of gratitude. “Thank you,” she said.

The woman grinned. "Name's Mercy. Everyone's always tellin' me I don't make enough of an effort to live up to it. You look like you could use a drink."

Alesa flinched and shook her head. "I don't drink."

"Well what could you use, then? Cup of coffee? Bowl of soup? A warm bath? Any or all of the above I'm offering, free of charge."

"You're very kind. I can't."

"*Kind,* my ass!" Mercy replied, and crouched down. "Look, honey, anyone could tell you're not from around these parts. Wouldn't take most a second glance. It's not safe for you to be out here alone. We've had a lot of girls go missing from these streets lately. And I mean a *lot.*"

"I'm not alone," Alesa said as she stood, pointing to the loudspeakers. "My father."

The sadness was plainly visible in Mercy's red and gold eyes when she said that. "Honey, if your father brought you out here... he's got to be damn mean or damn stupid."

Alesa nodded. "Yeah." She went down the stairs and stepped over Murphy, who still lay motionless, sprawled in a puddle. She looked back to Mercy, briefly, said "Thank you, again," and then was on her way, back through the crowds.

She found her father a little way from where she'd left him, still babbling to anyone within earshot about the wages of sin and the transforming power of the Savior's love.

***

Eight more days of preaching. Eight more days of enduring the abuse of strangers with her father's words wrapped around her shoulders. Alesa sought refuge where and when she could.

She was expected to wander away from her father, to spread his word, to hand out Bibles. She was able, for brief periods, to take shelter, seeking out moments of solace away from the crowds. After a few failed attempts, she was also able to imitate the action Mercy had shown her in disabling the loudspeakers. For spells she could hide out in the shadows, enjoying the peace and the solitude. She didn't feel *safe*... but then she very rarely did.

Though she warned herself to stay away, it was only a couple of days before she was back in the vicinity of the Weeping Worm, keeping an optimistic eye out for her silver angel. At first she was too worried about being spotted to stay for long. Then she discovered the cellar across the street – abandoned and accessed by a rusted door in the alley. Standing on an empty packing crate in its dank confines, she was able to peer out of the small window, past the ankles of the pedestrians in the thoroughfare, to the staircase where Mercy made her occasional appearances.

It was while she was standing at the window, gazing across at Mercy idly smoking a cigarette against the railings, that *he* introduced himself.

“I've seen that look a hundred thousand times...”

Alesa’s whole body tensed at the sound of his voice. Her balance faltered, but she gripped the window ledge and stayed standing.

“They call it... *envy*.”

She turned to peer through the darkness and saw the outline of two figures on the other side of the cellar. The sound of white phosphorus struck against brick was followed by a burst of violet light from the figure on the left. He held the match first to his pipe – illuminating a narrow, lined face and eyes hidden behind tinted spectacles – then used it to ignite a small paraffin lamp. When the wick was turned up it revealed a skinny, hump-backed man in a clear plastic raincoat. He had four thin arms, with fingers like stainless steel knitting needles, and a long, black tail like an alligator. He was, without question, one of the most frightening things she'd ever seen.

His cracked lips sucked long and hard on the end of the pipe, then let loose a great cloud of purple smoke as he said: “You're from the Damned part of town.”

Alesa said nothing. She was too afraid to move.

The smoker continued: "You don't have to confirm it. It's obvious. Bohren spotted you in the street from fifty yards away. Of course, he's always had an eye for the Damned girls, being native to that region himself."

Alesa's gaze moved to the man on the right – a varnished amalgam of sculpted teak and plaster in blue jeans and a butcher's apron. She recognized the scars on his neck, face and bald head as the markings of an Ellery Wynd healer. He stared back at her intensely, but said nothing.

With some considerable effort, and after a few halting gasps, Alesa managed to find her voice. "Wh— what do you want?"

The four-armed hunchback's lips twisted around the end of the pipe, forming a lopsided smile, utterly devoid of merriment or warmth. "Put simply, my dear, we'd like to offer you everything you've ever dreamed of."

***

He told her that his name was Dr. Lazzarin and that he was a remarkably gifted cosmetic surgeon. He also told her a few things about herself. "You are very ugly," he said. "Even here, in Grudgehaven, you must rank as one of the most visually unappealing creatures walking on two legs."

Alesa – who had never had much going for her in the self-esteem department – didn't even try to argue.

"I can change all that," Lazzarin said. "I can make you desirable, enviable... above all else, *beautiful.* I can do that. I assure you, I don't make empty promises."

"The Savior sees the beauty in all things," Alesa said. This was the best she could do in a tight corner. Trumpeting her father's nonsense.

"If he does, then he's the only one," Lazzarin countered. "What's that worth, weighed against the envy and adoration of the whole city? Would he love you any less?" The question hung in the air like so much tobacco smoke. Lazzarin had a long, thin tongue that flickered back and forth in his mouth whenever he wasn't talking. It moved and sounded like a rattlesnake's tail.

“Why are you offering this to me?” she asked.

“Because I see what others do not. Where they only see ugliness, I see potential. The clay that clings to your bones may be lumpen and grotesque, but it's all of a oneness. You've seen the girls on the streets here. By the time most of them are your age they've been broken apart and put together so many times and from so many different parts they're barely recognizable as female. Not you, though. No chop-shop half-measures for you.” He pointed with the end of his pipe, waving it up and down her body. “You're *pure.* All the right parts... just not necessarily in the right order. I can change that.” He motioned with both left arms towards Bohren. “*We* can change that. We can do remarkable things. Just ask Mercy.”

Though Alesa said nothing, the shock must have shown in her face, for Lazzarin grinned, leaving a gap between his teeth for his rattling tongue.

“What?” he said. “You think she was born that way? *No one* in the Grudge was born that way. We made her what she is. When she came to us she was just like you. Not as heavy, perhaps, but that's okay. Gives us more to work with.”

Alesa wasn't able to adequately process what they were offering. Her brain swam with the surreality of it all. She knew enough to say: “I can't. My father... And I've no money. I couldn't pay you.”

“That wouldn't be a concern.” Lazzarin said it like it was something he said all the time. “We could work out an arrangement. Beneficial to us both.”

“A what?”

“You'd pay us after the operation,” Bohren said. They were the first words he'd spoken during the entire exchange. “You'd make installments.”

Lazzarin snapped his teeth at the younger man, furious at him for speaking out of turn.

"How?" Alesa asked. "How would I do that?"

Turning back to her, Lazzarin forced another smile. "There are so many ways," he said, "for a beautiful young woman to earn a living."

***

It took almost twenty minutes for her to talk her way out of the cellar. Dr. Lazzarin's sales pitch was intense and well-practiced, but eventually she realized that was all it was – a pitch. Neither he nor Bohren had any other plans for her, she wasn't in immediate danger and was free to leave when she wished.

She did, but only after Lazzarin made her promise she would give their proposal "serious consideration."

"We have rooms in the basement of the Weeping Worm," he told her. "You can find us there." Bohren said nothing at all throughout the rest of the exchange, but his gaze never wandered from her for a moment.

Alesa found her father in Hazen Square some time later. She offered up all manner of apologies, making the vaguest of excuses for her long absence. Though he said nothing unkind, she could tell that he was seething.

When they were back in the hotel that evening, her worst fears were confirmed. His balled fist connected with the back of her head almost the moment she was through the door to her room. She was sent sprawling, chin-first onto the floor and bit through her tongue. He chased her down onto the floorboards, straddling her and raining blows down upon her back. She twisted under him, raised her hands to defend herself. He slapped them away and seized her neck, throttling her.

"Savior, grant me serenity," he wailed. "Savior, grant me patience." Green foam spilled from his lips and clung to his thick beard of tangled black wires. It was a sight she'd seen before, whenever he'd gone a week or more without alcohol. "Savior, grant me peace."

Just as the dots were beginning to dance at the edges of her vision, Alesa's father released his hold and stood. He took a deep, gasping breath, then crossed himself, closing his eyes and muttering: “By his grace, in his honor, in his name, for his love...”

Alesa didn't dare move. She lay where she'd fallen, sucking down the blood, though it hurt to swallow.

When he'd finished his prayer, her father opened his eyes and gazed down at her. There was no compassion in his stare. “You are my daughter. You will not leave my side again. You will not turn your back on the Savior's love and you will not dishonor me. This is not a warning, so do not test me.” He sniffed and ran a hand over his tired face. “Though I can hardly believe it, there appears to be a church not far from here. Many of the sinners today have been telling me so. They tell me they are members of the congregation, though I can scarcely believe it. We will go there tomorrow. We will speak to their priest and see what he has to say for himself. Our mission here is just beginning, Alesa. It is critical that we succeed. Bless his name before you go to bed.”

He left her room without another word, slamming the door behind him.

Alesa stayed where she was, lying bloodied and bruised across the floorboards and wondering to herself just what she must look like.

***

The Church of Zigguroth was a pink neon fortress – the throbbing heart of Paramour Park. Alesa's father's jaw dropped open at the sight of it and stayed that way till they were right up at the door. Once upon a time it probably had been a place of worship, but on being taken over by Caligula Zigguroth it had been transformed into a place of business. He'd clad the facade and steeple in fluorescent bulbs and swapped out the stained glass murals for ones that were a little more pornographic. On the inside he'd installed three bars, six stages and one enormous fountain in the middle of the floor. In Grudgehaven, the Church of Zigguroth was the premiere pleasure palace and the line to get in wound all the way around the block.

“No!” Alesa's father screamed as they crossed the street towards it. “No! Blasphemy!”

She clung desperately onto his arm, fearing anything less would be read as a sign of disloyalty. Fat drops of rain pelted heavily upon them, and claps of thunder sounded, almost like punctuation to her father's words.

“The ways of lust and debasement are a trap for the cowardly,” he cried as they approached the entrance. Price boards around the doors advertised cheap booze, cheap women and attractive combination deals. “Each return to the trough of adultery only weakens a man more and is like a knife in the Savior's very heart!”

“Can it, Crazy,” someone in the line yelled.

“Yeah,” said another. “Shut that stinkin' mouth before I shut it for you.”

Her father raised his Bible high over his head. “The way to his love cannot be divined through impurity. Malefactors condemn themselves to the pitiless void!”

“Now just hold on there!” A large, suited man stepped out from the entrance, his head hidden under a pink umbrella. “You better settle down, mister. I got nothin' against free speech, but you can't just come around here harassin' the clientele. It's bad for business.”

“Blasphemer!” Alesa's father pointed a crooked finger at the doorman. “I demand to speak with the owner of this affront to morality!”

The man chuckled. When he tilted the umbrella back, Alesa saw he had a long, sloping head with a horn protruding from the end of his snout. “Brother,” he said. “That's the *last* thing you want. Mr. Zigguroth doesn't have much patience for your kind. Even less than me.”

Alesa felt a hand clamp down on her shoulder. Turning her head, she saw that was exactly what it was – a severed hand. She shrieked.

“Don't worry about him,” said the man with the horn in his face. “He's with me.”

“You shan't silence us,” Alesa's father continued, again thrusting a finger in the man's face. “We are performing the Savior's work and we will stay here as long as it takes. I will preach in this very spot night and day. I will see this monstrosity crumble into dust!”

“You got a hell of an imagination,” the doorman said. His eyes fixed on Alesa's father's finger. He watched it shake for a while, then sighed. “Buddy, how long is it since you last had a drink?”

Alesa's father shrunk back in horror and withdrew his hand. “I... I haven't... I don't drink.”

The doorman smiled. “Sure you don't. Maybe that's your problem. How about you come inside and I fix you up with a couple shots? On the house.”

Alesa watched her father very carefully. She saw the usual rage and bluster in his features as he opened his mouth to reply... but then said nothing. She watched the same rage and bluster dissolve into sadness and exhaustion.

“I can't,” he said, wearily. “I shouldn't.”

“Sure you should,” the doorman said. “It'll do you good. Come on in out of the rain. Sit yourself down at the bar and I'll see if we can't get you that one-to-one with Mr. Z.”

Alesa's father licked his sandpaper lips. “Maybe... maybe just the one... to stiffen my resolve.” He moved forward, into the doorway, as the doorman's arm curled around him, guiding him through.

“Father!” Alesa called, the porcelain hand dancing a jig on her shoulder. “Father, wait!” She gave chase, but was halted as the doorman turned back and stuck out his arm.

“Sorry,” he said. “No can do. The padre's one thing, but...”

“He's my father,” Alesa pleaded. “I have to be by his side.”

The doorman put on the best approximation of a sympathetic smile he could. “I hate to do this to you, sweetheart, really I do. But I got a job to do and my boss has these rules... Y'see, this here's a pleasure palace. And a girl like you, lookin' the way you look... it's like the street preachin.' Just plain bad for business.”

He flicked a finger to the hand and it hopped across from her shoulder to his. Then the doorman turned and went back inside, leaving Alesa adrift on the sidewalk. Many of the patrons standing in line studied her for a few moments, each one clearly considering her worth. At the end of their contemplations they turned their heads to look elsewhere, their collective decision plain – she was worthless.

Alesa waited outside the Church of Zigguroth for close to thirty minutes, though she knew her father would not reappear for hours and, when he did, would probably be too drunk to recognize her. Shivering from the rain, in desperate need of shelter, she finally forced herself down the street, and rounded the corner onto 35th. It was here that a black town car drew up alongside her, its window lowered, the driver a vague outline in shadow. He said nothing and Alesa said nothing to him. He regarded her the same way the people in line had, then wound his window up and continued on his way.

Alesa halted, remembering Mercy's words about girls "going missing" on these streets, then broke into a run and didn't stop till she reached the Weeping Worm. She charged up the iron stairs and threw herself through the doors, then stood there, dripping rainwater on the sawdust and gasping for air. Luckily, Mercy, standing at the bar, was the first one to notice her.

"Sweetie?" she said, putting down her drink and crossing the floor towards her. "You okay?"

"The drink," Alesa gasped. "The soup. The bath... Still on offer?"

***

She washed in good hot water and dried out first, then ate sitting up at the bar. Mercy joined her. They talked about Alesa's father, about Old Town and about each other. Eventually, inevitably, somebody brought up the subject of Dr. Lazzarin.

"Oh sure, he can do everything he says," Mercy said, twirling a black cigarette between her fingers. "He'll turn you into a firecracker of a doll, if you let him. A real piece of work. But it ain't exactly a bowl of cherries. You know that, right?"

“You came here from the Old Town, didn't you?” Alesa said.

Mercy nodded. “I lived there, once upon a time. With my old face and my old name.”

“Bohren. He's from the Old Town, too. Ellery Wynd.”

“You're a sharp one.” Mercy placed the cigarette between her smiling lips and struck a match. “Bohren followed me here. The two of us were betrothed at one time. You know the way it works. I didn't like the idea, so I ran, ended up here. Lazzarin found me and offered the same deal he's offering you. And I took it. Couple years later, Bohren tracked me down. I don't think he knew me, not at first. But I couldn't hide the fact I knew him... and that tore it.”

“Why didn't he take you back?” Alesa asked. “It was his right.”

“After all I'd done – and *had* done – to myself, he didn't want me. Not the Ellery Wynd way. But he couldn't go home empty handed. His people are weird that way. So he stuck around. He'd spent his whole life training to be a healer, which made him the perfect apprentice for Lazzarin. And so...” She spun circles with her fingers, indicating the rest was fairly self-explanatory. “When they presented themselves to you, did they say what they'd want in return?”

Alesa shrank down in her seat. “Not exactly. But I think I can guess.”

“Well let me spell it out for you,” Mercy said, reaching for a bottle and pouring herself a fresh measure of absinthe. “Lazzarin ain't just a doc. He's a pimp. You'll pay him back one trick at a time. When it's not tricks, it'll be parties, dirty movies, pictures... a world of sleaze and degradation. And it'll take *years*. I mean... even if you thought you were the hardest working whore in the business – and I don't reckon you are, nor could be – for every trick you turn, Lazzarin gets a cut. And bein' that he's got to pay Zigguroth for the spot, and Zigguroth pays the King of Eyes for the franchise, and tricks never pay much in the first place, that cut's gonna be pretty big. You'll work your no-doubt pretty little ass off every week just to break even. Look at me!” She raised her glass in mock toast. “I've been here six years now. I'm beginning to come to terms with the idea I ain't ever gettin' out. On the other hand, even I'll admit I look pretty damn good." She knocked the shot back and licked a drop of emerald liquor from her glistening lips. "You've got to ask yourself if you think it's worth it."

Alesa stared across the bar to the mirror on the back wall. She'd avoided looking at it since entering – the same way she tried to ignore all reflections of herself – but she gave herself a good hard stare now. She studied the misshapen outline of her head, tapering into a knot of greasy hair and bone at the top. She saw the large, square forehead and her own small, black eyes blinking on either side of a pig-like snout. Saw her crooked teeth, heavy jowls and double chin, folding over the neck of a frayed flower-pattern dress. When she let herself imagine how it might feel to peer into a mirror and see a face like Mercy's looking back at her, she thought she might explode into tears.

Instead, she cleared her throat and, in a very quiet voice, said: "If I stay with my father, eventually he'll kill me or he'll get me killed. I have no money to go anywhere else and as long as I have this face he will *always* find me. Every night, for as long as I can remember, I've prayed to the Savior for a way out. And this *is* a way out."

Staring sadly into the bottom of her glass, Mercy shrugged and replied: "Well... sounds like you've made your choice."

***

Lazzarin made no effort to conceal his delight. In the brief moments he wasn't speaking, his tongue sliced through the tobacco smoke like a chopping blade. His long, coiling tail began to wag slowly from side to side and his second pair of hands rubbed against each other with feverish enthusiasm. Bohren, sitting on a stool in the corner, arms folded, said nothing and did nothing. If Alesa thought she saw any expression on his stoic face, she'd say it was probably one of disappointment.

The deal was made in Lazzarin's basement surgery, hidden underneath the Weeping Worm. It was much as Mercy had described. At the moment Alesa emerged from the Doc's chrysalis as a beguiling feminine goddess, she would be worth millions. As the physical embodiment of a concept most Grudgehaven citizens were utterly unable to grasp, she would be highly sought after. Men – and women – across the city and from every social sphere would amputate and sell their own body parts just to get close to her. This was what Lazzarin predicted. Her beauty would outstrip even Mercy's, he said.

“A sketch,” he said. “A half-assed scrawl compared to you. We've made a lot of progress since Mercy, Bohren and I. We've perfected our processes and invented new ones. We've been able to *improve* the odd girl here and there, but till you we never had the ideal canvas. Your unfortunate body, my dear, is the clay from which we will create a masterpiece!”

As such, she would be expected to bring in the cash, using what she'd been given to *pay* for what she'd been given. As long as it took.

“And don't think you'll be able to pick and choose your johns,” Mercy warned her. “However you choose to play it, the Doc will be first in line for a taste. And you'll have to give it to him. However many times he wants it.”

They went through a detailed explanation of the surgery. The Doc expected it to take around twelve days, possibly longer, but promised she would be too doped up to know or care. He explained that he would be responsible for most of the bone realignment and full bodywork – all the most difficult stuff. Bohren would handle the finer cosmetic touches, putting in the delicate details around her eyes, lips and hands. When asked if she had any preferences, Alesa told them: “Blue. I want to be blue.”

They all agreed. They shook hands. Alesa was shown to a room on the third floor and advised by Mercy to get some rest.

Hours later, after closing, she tiptoed back downstairs, found the door to Bohren's room and gave it a little tap. When he answered, she said: “Mind if I come in?”

***

“Sincerely... I am humbled by my own genius.” Lazzarin wasn't kidding. His spectacles had clouded over. As he removed them, Alesa saw a thick black tear ooze down his cheek.

She was encased from neck to foot in an amber resin – the same kind healers in Old Town used to repair serious cuts, blisters and other skin damage. She'd never seen it used in such quantities and had to guess Bohren had secured a steady supply that they'd been stockpiling for years. It had formed a hard crust over her body and made it impossible to move.

The Doc had begun the process of setting her free, but only made it as far as peeling the bandages and gelatin mask from her face before he had to stop, finding himself totally overcome with emotion.

"Wonderful..." His hand was shaking as it reached out towards her, needle-tipped fingers quivering just an inch from her perfect cheekbones. "Simply wonderful."

"Please," she said, with a mouth that didn't feel like her own. "Get me out of here."

Bohren stepped in then, using a circular saw to make calculated incisions in the resin's tough exterior. He didn't look her in the eye.

"The price will have to go up," Lazzarin said, his breaths getting rapid as the resin was snapped away in large, crumbling chunks. "Across the board. That's all there is to it. They'll *have* to go up." He laughed. "My word, Alesa, we can't let Mercy ever see you. The poor girl will feel ugly all over again."

"I want to see," Alesa said. Her strange new tongue pressed against unfamiliar teeth. "Please. I have to see."

The Doc nodded eagerly and slithered away into a corner of the cluttered laboratory as Bohren liberated her left arm from its crystal cage. She raised it to her face and couldn't quite believe what she was seeing. Smooth and delicate, like frosted glass, fair of complexion with a subtle blue tint. Not one mark, blemish or wrinkle. No unsightly seams, no creaking joints, no exposed wires. Her flawless fingers ended in nails of deep blue.

When Bohren had cut enough away, she stepped out of the collapsed husk and into the middle of the floor. Lazzarin placed a long, cracked mirror in front of her and watched delightedly as a brilliant smile burst across her face.

“That's not me,” she said, reaching a hand out towards her naked reflection. “It can't be.”

She was staring into stunning blue eyes – the same color as her nails. Her long hair, lips and nipples were all the same engineered shade. She turned her body, studying its new shape, seeing the way its lines curved and discovering wonderful new contours. When the vision blurred, she looked back to her strange, adorable face and saw that tears of deep blue were pouring from her eyes.

“I'm beautiful,” she wept.

“Yes,” Lazzarin answered, while his tongue chattered. “You are.”

Bohren said nothing.

The Doc held out a handkerchief and she took it gratefully, dabbing at her eyes. “It's too much,” she said. “I never imagined... I *couldn't* have imagined...”

“There, there,” said the Doc, putting a sympathetic claw on her bare shoulder. His tail – seemingly of its own accord – had curled towards her and was now rubbing against her leg. “You've no good reason to cry. Not anymore.”

“You're right.” She nodded, sniffed and blinked the tears away, then turned her eyes on him. “I should be thanking you. I very nearly said I didn't know *how* to thank you... but I don't think that's true...” She stepped into his arms and pressed her lips against his.

He responded with surprise at first, then hunger, wrapping his limbs around her and slipping his thin, quivering tongue into her mouth. She felt it twitching against her own tongue, felt it dancing with erotic excitement... felt it freeze.

Lazzarin broke the kiss after just a few seconds and stepped back, his face a haunted map of confusion. “No,” he said, as his arms turned inwards, hands pawing at his heart. He looked to Alesa, his eyes hot with anger and fear. “NO!” He shuddered, then collapsed against an instrument table and crashed to the floor, where he lay, convulsing uncontrollably.

Alesa watched him, saying nothing and making no movements till he lay twitching at her feet. At that point, she pinched her bottom lip between thumb and forefinger and peeled away the thin – almost invisible – sliver of adhesive gum Bohren had planted, laced with extract of Locust's Kiss. She rolled it up in her fingers and flicked it away.

“Y'know,” Alesa said, “I almost feel bad about this. Almost. Fact is, Doc... it just wasn't a very good deal.”

Lazzarin's teeth were grinding hard against each other. She could hear them squeak. He stared up at her, expression full of hate and pain, unable to respond but comprehending every word.

Alesa leaned towards him. “Y'see, what I like about *this* deal is that I didn't have to sleep with every man in the Grudge. Just one.” She pointed to Bohren, lurking somewhere on the other side of the room. “*Him*. See, one thing I know about Ellery Wynders that you may not – being as how you're not from the Old Town – is that they value purity above everything else. Clearly, thanks to you, Bohren had lost his way. But I went to him and was able to remind him of his oaths and set him back on the path. I suppose, if you wanted to, you could call it a sermon of sorts. I helped him see that it was time for him to atone for all his sins... and time for you to die.”

Lazzarin's face had drained of color. He stuck out his jaw and puckered his lips in a desperate attempt to speak. “You...” he choked. “You... You...”

“Oh, I know.” Alesa grinned. “I'm a real piece of work.”

Lazzarin wheezed, his fingers scratching at the cement as his body seized up. He gave a great sigh, spraying spittle across the floor, then rolled onto his back, shivered and went still.

Alesa stepped over his body to reach the lab coat hanging on a hook on the wall. She went into the pocket, found a pair of coins, then crouched down and placed them over his eyes.

***

Bohren said it would be easy to get rid of the Doc's body. They had drums of acid concealed in a small store-room next to the lab. He assured her he'd handle it himself before heading back to Ellery Wynd.

“I'm sure you've got time for more than that,” she cooed, pressing her body up against his. “How about it?”

“Only pure,” he said, shoving her away. “Only virgins.”

She was stunned into silence for a moment, then laughed, replying: “Well I guess I'm not either of those anymore. Thanks to you.”

Mercy had provided some of her least-favorite garments. Alesa was now slimmer and taller than her silver idol – with a much smaller bust size – but she was able to cobble together enough for an outfit.

She didn't let anyone else in the Weeping Worm see her. She didn't want anyone else to know that her face – the most beautiful in the Grudge – had once belonged to ugly Alesa, the Preacher's daughter. She considered her new identity as she strode proudly down the street, quietly enjoying the stunned faces of those who caught sight of her, and decided, after some consideration, that her name was Sel.

Sel didn't know where she was going or what she would do when she got there, but she was unafraid, bolstered by the Doc's own assurance that there were so many ways for a beautiful young girl to earn a living.

“Alesa!”

She froze, unsure at first where the cry had come from.

“Alesa!” There was a man up ahead, weaving his way through the crowd. By the time she realized it was her father it was too late to get out of his way. “Alesa!” He was screaming the name at anyone who passed by him, walking up to them and shouting: “My daughter! Have you seen her? I need to find her... I... I have to... Alesa! Alesa!”

She started walking, meaning to pass him by without a glance, pretend she had never seen him before.

“Alesa!”

It wasn't possible. As they came alongside one another, she turned her head towards him. Their eyes met.

“I'm looking for my daughter,” he told her. “She's lost. Alone. She needs me!”

Sel shook her head and said nothing.

The preacher glared at her with wide-eyed frustration, then turned away. “Alesa! Alesa, where are you? Alesa!” He called again and kept calling as he pressed on, then disappeared into the crowd.

Sel, a moment later, did the same.

One Parasite to Another

Frank sat in a pew close to the front in the Creeping Vine Chapel, staring at a hanging statue of the Savior on the Cross. It was an orthodox depiction of the Savior, rendered in gold and stainless steel. More revisionist interpretations saw him in plastic and rubber. It was argued that he must have been made of weaker stuff, or his aggressors would never have got the nails through his hands and feet, nor the spear into his side. Most churchgoers – including the Creeping Vine's congregation – found the very idea offensive in the extreme.

Frank saw a lot of himself in the Savior's face: the long, drawn features, pointed chin and flat, shapeless nose. The resemblance was there, too, in the expression. His was the visage of a man hunted, wounded and dying. Frank could empathize.

"Are you in need of counsel, my son?"

Frank hadn't heard the clergyman approach, nor felt the shifting of the pew as he sat down. His senses were beginning to fail him.

He turned awkwardly around, trying to hide the pain it was causing him, and came face-to-face with a thin man in the robes of a young priest. The skin on his neck and around his eyes looked brown and cracked, like a desert road, but was mostly hidden by a mask of carved ivory.

"You know what they say, padre," Frank said. His voice sounded like a boot heel mashing gravel. "Only fools come clean. But how good are you at performing Last Rites?"

"As good as any other." The priest's lips moved behind a pattern of small holes cut into the mask. "Are you unwell?"

"You could say that..." Frank peeled open the right side of his leather jacket and showed the priest his bullet holes. The blood that leaked from the ragged wounds glimmered like petroleum and reeked like rotten eggs.

The priest gagged from the sudden stench, then leaped to his feet, signaling to one of the altar boys.

“My God, man. We must get you a doctor.”

“No.” Frank grabbed the man by the wrist and pulled him back down, surprised to find he still had the strength. “No doctors. No cops. They find me now and I'll end up in a place worse than Hell.”

“There might be time yet,” the priest urged. “The wounds...”

“Will kill me,” Frank interrupted. “You can let the rest of the world know then. You can tell 'em all. Once I'm dead. Not before. Right now, what I need... is just a place to sit. Till I die.”

The priest shook his head. “This is madness.”

“You wouldn't say that if you knew... Knew who I was.” The world was beginning to sway around him. He felt a weighty warmth rising through his body.

“I can hazard a guess,” the priest said. “Some kind of mobster, bank robber, murderer. You've come too late to seek forgiveness here.”

“Please...” Frank's wet fingers fumbled for the chain at his neck, pulling a silver cross from his shirt. It was almost an identical match for the one the priest wore. “I'm a believer. I'm a believer, like you. I seek the Savior's protection.”

The priest shook his head, sadly. “You ask too much of me.”

“Please... I'm begging you... Just let me sit here a while. Let me die.”

“I don't understand. Who are you?”

Frank slumped towards the priest, squeezing his hand around his wrist. “Please. I'm carrying a lot of sin and a lot of secrets. Just... say a prayer for me, Father. Put in a word... if you can... with the man upstairs.”

The priest leaned in close, frowning behind his mask. “And who should I tell him it's for?”

“Tell him I'll be there soon...” Frank couldn't feel his mouth moving, but he could hear his own words echoing back to him. “Tell him it's Frank... Tell him... it's the King... of Broken Glass...”

And with that, came darkness.

***

When Frank was a boy, making his way in the world fishing for dead bodies along Fester's River and stripping them of whatever he could sell, he'd seen his best friend taken by a cluster-shark.

It had happened under a footbridge north of the ED. Kolbi, the kid Frank was closest to and had known most of his young life, led the way, hopping across stepping stones to an area where the stream dipped into a bend, half-covered by strips of metal. Though it was awkward to get to, you were usually guaranteed a catch if you made the effort. This day was no different. The orange lamplight in the center of Kolbi's face lit up a fat vinyl man, sitting half out of the water. He looked like a suicide, wrapped up in ropes tied to rocks, but his tweed jacket had snagged on the metal splinters, trapping him in the bend before the current could carry him into deeper waters. He'd likely died in agony, smashed up against the wall by passing debris.

To the kids it was just another score. Kolbi couldn't reach the dead man with his hands. He had to reach out over the torrent with a stick to flick open the man's lapel and hook the chain of his silver pocket watch.

“Look at this, Frank,” he said, grinning back over his shoulder. “We're rich!”

That was when the shark got him.

Most people in the Grudge had never even heard of cluster-sharks. Even to the pickpockets on Fester's River they were little more than legend. You just didn't expect that kind of crazy shit north of the Damned. But there were some that claimed to have seen their carbuncle bodies twisting just below the water's surface, or caught sight of a spiked fin splashing in the froth. Some said heavy rains washed Blacklands slime into the river from the North and sometimes a little blob of slime would get churned up with whatever pieces of plastic, metal and feces happened to be around, get confused, and start acting like fish. Over time it would collide with more scrap, more trash, more broken bodies, assuming it all and reforming itself till it was one monstrous mess of disease, teeth and fury. Some people liked to theorize that was how all life in the Grudge started out. And some people needed to be locked away for their own good.

Like most kids his age, Frank enjoyed the stories, but never believed them. Not till the moment he saw its warped metal body arc out of the foam to clamp its jaws around his friend's arm and drag him down to the depths.

That moment had stayed with him throughout his life, remained vivid in every nightmare and unwelcome flashback. He saw its gruesome face, turned towards him, misshapen teeth set wide and bearing down as Kolbi screamed. He saw it now, floating through the air towards him. Heard Kolbi's desperate cry...

It was only when he threw up a weak hand and saw it pass through the shark's body that he realized it was a hallucination. It faded slowly – though not immediately – from his vision as his arm dropped back to the bed. The echoing cries for help did not cease, however. It took a few seconds before Frank realized they did not belong to his long-dead friend, but an altar boy, standing in the doorway.

"Father!" the altar boy called. "Father Cisero! Come quickly! He's awake!"

***

"How do you feel?" Cisero asked, peering through the holes in his mask. He sat on the bed beside Frank. The kid stood behind him, pretending not to pay attention. He had a thick neck and a flat head, with spiraling clear plastic tubes sprouting from the top, bending down into his back. A cheap cross of battered tin was pinned to his chest. In another life, Frank thought, he'd have fit right in along the river.

"I feel like I ought to be dead," Frank answered. They were in a small room made of gray stone, with one small window in the corner and no furniture but the bed and a sideboard. Fairly typical quarters for a man of the cloth.

“You might perish yet,” the priest said. He rolled back the sheets to examine the patch-up job he'd made of the bullet wounds, then tapped a finger against the beakers hanging above the bed, attached to Frank's wrist by a drip. They were filled with a pale yellow sludge. “I wasn't sure exactly what your constitution required,” he continued. “I had to make a few guesses. With any luck you may be back on your feet in... say... three weeks.”

“How have you managed this?” Frank asked.

“I've picked up the odd skill here and there. I've done my best. You'd probably still have been better off in a hospital. Then again... maybe not.”

Frank smirked, ignoring the pain it caused him. “So you *have* heard of me.”

Cisero looked to the altar boy, still trying to make it look like he wasn't listening, then turned back to Frank. “Everyone's heard of the King of Broken Glass,” he said. “I have a mobster or two in my congregation. They keep me updated. They say you're dead.”

“That's what Eyes wants everyone to think.” Frank sneered. “Makes him look weak if the whole city knows he botched the job. But if all the Grudge is convinced he marked my card, then they'll all fall into line like good little toy soldiers.”

“I suppose they'll be looking for you.”

“Some,” he admitted. “The ones that know.”

Cisero nodded. And there was something about the *way* he nodded that Frank didn't like. Though he couldn't see his face, he got the idea there was a smile on it that spelled trouble.

“You should rest,” Cisero said as he stood, then crossed to the door. “Have faith. Three weeks and you'll be right as rain. You're quite safe here.”

Frank knew, then, that he had to get out as soon as he could.

***

The kid said his name was Raphael. He brought Frank his meals when he was well enough to eat, plus a few pills after he came off the drip. There were other altar boys in the chapel. Raphael admitted as much and Frank sometimes heard their voices and running footfalls in the corridor outside his room, but he never saw them. The circumstances suggested Cisero had kept his patient a secret from all but Raphael.

This was a good thing. It meant that, when he escaped, Frank would need to kill fewer people to cover his tracks. And they *had* to die, there was no question about that. Frank was a man hunted, despised, his armies food for crows. He had to be vicious to survive. He had to be practical. In a way, he was looking forward to the challenge. It would be more like the old days, the good old bad times, doing all his own killing and clinging to the shadows. He couldn't afford sentimentality. The kid had to die. Presuming he knew who he was.

“You know who I am?” he asked after a week of the kid setting a tray before him.

Raphael avoided his eyes at first, shaking his head, then slowly looked up and answered: “You're the King of Broken Glass.”

Frank nodded, unable to resist a smile. “You're damn right.”

“You've killed men,” the boy continued, in awe.

“A great many,” Frank confirmed.

“You've lied, cheated and doomed others to lives of chaotic villainy.”

“That's just the Cliff Notes.”

“You're a devil.”

“No.” Frank raised his finger and waved it back and forth. “Just a man.”

Raphael started the walk back to the door, keeping his eye on the bed, then stopped. “Father Cisero says we must help you. For the good of the church.”

Frank pulled himself up against the headboard. “He say anything else about me?”

The kid thought for a moment, then nodded. “He says you can't be trusted.” He closed the door after leaving the room.

Frank waited, listening to the footsteps receding down the hall, then shifted the tray from his lap, threw back the sheets and climbed out of bed.

He was healing quickly. Much more quickly than Cisero had guessed. He'd hastened the pace of his own recovery as much through sheer will as through the long bouts of painful exercise he'd subjected himself to whenever they'd left him alone long enough. Now, at last, he felt ready.

He limped into the far corner and stretched towards the small window. The view confirmed he was in the chapel's cellar, staring out across the cobbled and walled rear yard. It offered nothing of any use to him. He tried the door, but it didn't open. It didn't surprise him that they would lock him in, for his own sake if for no one else's, but for the first time he noticed a small hatch at eye-level, impossible to slide open from his side. That concerned him.

He inspected every inch of the room, but uncovered nothing that would aid in his escape. Finally, he concluded his only option would be to strike when Raphael made his next visit.

He returned to bed and ate his meal – stew in a wooden bowl, with a wooden spoon. When he was finished, he snapped the spoon, making a half-decent – if short – stake. It wasn't much of a weapon, but, if used correctly, could be of some value. He concealed it under the sheets, lay back and waited.

Night fell. The dawn came. Raphael did not. His next meal was delivered through a hatch.

“What's going on?” Frank called, putting on a feeble voice. “Who's there? I... I can't see...”

“If you want to eat, you'd better come get it.” The voice was Cisero's. “Come on. I know you can walk, Frank.”

“Walk? The Hell you talkin' about? I can barely feel my legs.”

“This is how it has to be from now on. You're not fully recovered, but you're well enough to be a threat. I won't put myself – or any of my boys – in harm's way.”

Frank sighed. The guy was a smart one. “Fine,” he said, dropping all pretense of invalidity. “So when do I get out of here?”

“Like I said. After three weeks, you should be back at peak physical condition. Exactly how the King of Eyes wants you.”

“What?” Frank bolted upright. “What do you mean?” He rolled out of bed, moving so fast he almost pitched forward on his weak leg, but stayed upright. He snatched up the stake and hobbled towards the door. “Answer me!”

The priest chuckled somewhere Frank couldn't see him. “Exactly what I said. You're still too weak to go to the King of Eyes. If he put you in his wall now, you'd last... what? A week? Maybe two? No, he'll want better than that. He'll want to make you suffer for centuries if he can. So you'll stay here till you're all better. Don't worry. It won't be long.”

“Son of a bitch. You son of a bitch! You've been working for him all this time?”

“Hardly. I'm a servant of God, Frank, not of kings. But imagine what Eyes will pay when he learns you've been captured alive. Imagine how many poor souls could be helped with that cash.”

“Bullshit,” Frank spat. “Servant of God my ass! You're serving yourself, you sack of shit. Nothing but a god-damn parasite is what you are.”

Cisero laughed at that. Actually laughed. “Very good, Frank. I suppose you ought to know. What do you care what I do with the money? Either way you're finished. Enjoy the meal. While you still can.”

Frank heard his footsteps retreating down the hall and screamed: “Wait! Stop! Please!”

“Sorry, Frank,” he called.

“Please! I'll pay you. More than him! More than you could ever spend! You can have it all! You can have it all!”

Cisero halted. Doubled back. Frank saw a portion of his face appear on the other side of the hatch. “All of what?” he said, meaning it as an insult. “In case you haven't noticed, Frank, you're done. All your men are dead. All your money is gone. Eyes looked at what you had, took what he wanted and torched the rest. That's what he does.”

“Not all of it,” Frank said, sounding more desperate by the moment. “There was a stash he didn't know about. A stash nobody knew about but me. While Eyes was spending all his dough on fancy decorators and blimps, I was spending what I had to on muscle and putting the rest away. It's still there, where nobody is gonna find it. More money than you could count in two lifetimes. It's all there. Trust me.”

“Hmmm,” said Cisero. “Where?”

“Let me out of here. I'll show you.”

“No. You tell me where. I'll go check it out, and if it is what you say it is, we can renegotiate.”

“Damn you!” Frank yelled, slamming his fist against the door. “This isn't a game!”

“If it were, you'd be on the losing side,” the priest said, clearly unfazed. “Face it, Frank. What options do you have here? You want me to trust you? That works both ways.”

“Okay.” Frank breathed deeply, forcing himself to calm down. “Okay. But you've got to promise me that you'll let me out of here. When you have it, you keep it, take it, hide it, do whatever you like with it, but then you *let me out.* Got it?"

"Sure thing, pal." A big grin spread across Cisero's invisible face. "Anything else?"

Dejected, Frank let out a great sigh and shrugged. "A pack of smokes might be nice."

***

Truth was, Cisero had been hearing rumors of Frank's secret fortune for years. It was in a vault or a safety deposit box or an old mattress in an abandoned building. A lot of Frank's men had their theories. And a lot of Frank's men told Cisero.

A huge percentage of the repeat visitors to the Creeping Vine were gangsters. They needed to unburden themselves of the guilt of their abhorrent deeds. Cisero offered absolution... and remembered all he was told.

There was a church-owned truck – rarely used – stored in a garage down the street. Cisero peeled off the tarp, filled it with gas and, after a few false starts, was on his way north, following Frank's directions to the letter.

In less than two hours he was into the hills, weaving between the fortified homes of the Grudge's wealthier families, dreaming about which one would be his when this was all over. Frank's fortune alone would be more than enough, but he didn't plan to stop there. There was still the reward to come from the King of Eyes when he gave the good word.

And then, when he'd totted up his millions... there would be wine. There would be women and song and crazed carnal indulgence. After a lifetime wasted in abstinence he would bathe his whole body in vice. The thoughts made him so giddy he almost missed his turn.

Frank's map led beyond the outskirts of the city and into the forests just shy of the mountains. Cisero knew he'd reached his destination when he passed between two concrete lions and arrived at a palatial manor house, shrouded in darkness.

He chapped the heavy door and was answered almost immediately.

"And what would you want?" The man who stood in the doorway had only half a face. Cisero didn't care to wager how he'd lost the other half.

"Frank sent me," he said.

The man squinted with his one bleary eye. "Frank's dead."

Cisero sighed. "Then does it really matter?"

The man considered a moment, stroking a bony finger across what remained of his chin, then said: "I guess no, prob'ly not. But you still got to pay."

Cisero emptied his wallet impatiently. "Here."

"Not enough."

"Fine." He took off his rings and wristwatch, holding them out.

"Still not enough."

"I don't have anything else!"

The man pointed to the silver cross around his neck. "That."

Cisero hesitated a moment, then sighed. "Fine." He unhooked the chain and held it out. "Will that do?"

The half-faced man held the items up for inspection, tilted the cross in the light, then waved him through. "You better know where you're going. 'Cause I ain't helpin' you."

On the other side of the door, Cisero could see the manor house for what it truly was – a facade. There were no floors, no rooms, no elegant furnishings. Only the front wall and windows; a plywood construct propped up with timber beams. It was a theatrical, over-elaborate disguise to conceal something really quite mundane. Cisero stepped out of the stage scenery shadow and found himself on the edge of a limestone quarry, carved into the side of the mountain.

The site had been abandoned long ago – the cherished rock sold off to industry – and had flooded with half a decade of rain. The water shone like liquid emerald in the moonlight.

Cisero walked around the artificial lake's shore till he reached a long, poorly-made pier, jutting out across the water like a splinter in a green eyeball. Minding his footing – and making a few muttered prayers to a deity he didn't honestly believe in – he edged towards the end of the pier, where forty taut steel cables cut down into the icy depths. The lines were attached to a rusting winch and crank system – a handle for every line.

Cisero was aware of the half-faced goon watching him from the shoreline as he reached for the seventeenth handle from the left. "Only the seventeenth from the left," Frank had told him, being patronizingly emphatic. "All the others are booby trapped so don't touch 'em. You've got to be absolutely sure." If Cisero wasn't the first to come here, it was likely the goon had seen others meet a nasty fate at the end of this pier and was hoping to catch one more. If he *was* the first, then the guy was long overdue some entertainment.

"Sorry to disappoint," he muttered to himself, as he turned the crank handle and began reeling in the line. It came up slowly, almost reluctantly, its length stained black and slick with vegetation. Cisero kept on the job till it was all the way in, till he heard a crunch from the cable that told him it'd go no further. That done, he took a moment to catch his breath, then straightened up and examined his prize catch.

It was a box. A small – *very* small – metal box.

Cisero sighed, imagining Frank laughing from his cell back at the chapel. Before the box was in his hands his mind was racing ahead with all the possible outcomes. Most likely he'd find a key, probably to a safe deposit box somewhere in the city. And Frank would tell him, "They'll only admit me, with my face, my signature, but that's okay. Let me out of here and we'll go together. I'll split it with you."

There were four metal catches on the box. Snapping them open one by one, Cisero imagined the look on the King of Broken Glass' face when he told him: "No. Go screw yourself. We're done."

Grinning to himself, he flipped open the lid.

Sitting in the bottom of the box was a glistening gray blob. Cisero didn't know what it was. It looked like something a disease-ridden man might hawk up onto the sidewalk. He was about ready to dismiss it as exactly that – a crude, pointless joke by a petty, deposed tyrant – when he caught a sudden shiver of movement. That was all he caught before it hit him in the chest and knocked him down.

Cisero cracked his skull on the boards and felt the air go out of his lungs. Blinking through the pain he saw the gray thing prone on his chest. It had sprouted legs. Long, thin tendrils of hardened mucus that had pierced his body and whipped between his ribs. He let out a gasp of fright and disgust and tried to pull the creature away. Its skin burned to the touch, loosing more fibrous coils that slithered around his fingers and dug into his palm. He pulled his hands away almost immediately, but found they'd already been infected. They bristled with a moving map of pulsating purple veins.

He kicked his legs, rolling towards the water as the beast stretched its body, forming a bulbous head on the end of a long neck. Cisero felt its wet kiss below his jaw and the first stab of its teeth as he tipped over the side of the pier and sank like a stone into the lake.

Frank's half-faced employee, who had been enjoying the gruesome spectacle from the sidelines, now produced a pocket-watch and began to count the seconds as they ticked by – an activity he indulged in more for his own amusement than anything else. He noted the passing of four minutes and twenty-six seconds before the next ripple of movement glanced on the water's surface... and something that had once been a priest dragged itself slowly out onto the shore.

***

Raphael was not responsible for the candles. A wall of candles was lit in the chapel every evening after the doors were bolted – a tribute in the Savior's name – and Raphael had performed the task a great many times. However, he now had other, more important duties. He had graduated through the ranks and palmed the tedious job off on a younger boy by the name of Kovick.

When he entered the nave and found the candles unlit his first instinct was to strike a match and light them. He quashed that impulse as quickly as he could, reminding himself there was a hierarchy for a reason and that if Kovick couldn't carry out the simplest of chores he would have to be disciplined.

“Kovick!” Raphael marched down the aisle, peering down the empty pews. “Kovick!” He called again and heard a clattering noise from behind the pulpit. “You can't hide from me over there,” he said as he approached. “You come out of there now. Unless you want me to report this to Father Cis—” He froze as a small round shape shot up from behind the pulpit, flying high into the air and crashing down to land with a wet *THWAK* at his feet.

It was Kovick's head.

Raphael stared a long while at the mangled shape, unable to comprehend what he was seeing. When he turned back to the pulpit his gaze was met by a creature wearing the Father's shattered mask.

It stood on two legs, body a throbbing mess of dark, dripping sinews. Its twitching, ragged arms ended in large claws, steeped in the younger boy's bodily fluids. The eyes behind Cisero's ivory were dark and furious, while the mouth, fully exposed, hung wide open, revealing row upon row of blood-red metal teeth.

***

Frank sat with his back to the door, listening to the screams. The death of a child... The *violent* death of a child... It was horrible. He knew that. He understood.

But he couldn't resist a smile.

When the echoing cries at last ceased, he lit a cigarette and waited for Cisero to arrive. He didn't have to wait long.

Before the cigarette had burned all the way down he heard the slamming of doors in the corridor outside his room, the pounding of heavy feet and the sound of clenched claws smashing against the wall.

"Enjoying yourself?" he called.

"What have you done to me?" The voice that answered was not quite Cisero's. It was distorted, like his vocal chords had been fed into a grinder. He sounded exhausted, scared and very angry.

Frank took a final drag then flicked the butt into the far corner. "Honestly?" he said. "I don't know. You find all kinds of crazy shit when you go poking around the Blacklands. That's all my secret stash ever was. No money. Just those... *things.* But they're worth a lot in their own way. Consider that one a gift to you. One parasite to another."

The priest hammered his fists against the door. "Damn you! Damn you, it hurts! IT HURTS!!!"

"I'm sure it does," Frank chuckled. "I bet you've got a thirst that burns so bad you think it'll melt you from the inside if you don't quench it. I bet every muscle in your body is itching to kill."

He heard rasping close, just a few inches behind his head.

"Hate to tell you this," he continued. "Butchering all the little altar boys in the world won't slake that thirst for more than a minute."

"What do I do?" Cisero wheezed. "Please. Please tell me. What do I do?"

"What do you think you do? You let me the hell out of here. That's what you do."

"And you'll... you'll what?" He wept. "You'll cure me? Make me whole again?"

"I only know of one cure," Frank said. "But I'll share it with you, if you let me out."

He heard the priest straightening up, his spiked tendrils slapping wetly against the door. "If you try anything... I'll kill you."

Frank hauled himself up onto his feet, struggling a little with his bad leg. He brushed down his shirt front and took a few steps back. "I'll take my chances."

Bolts slid back and the door swung open. He saw what remained of the priest in all his blood-drenched glory. He filled the doorway, claws twitching, eager to tear the other man to pieces.

"There," he rasped. "Now cure me."

Frank looked Cisero up and down, then nodded. "When I was a boy, I saw my best friend killed by a cluster-shark. That's a close relation to the creature you let out of its box this evening. When I returned to the crypt we shared with a gang of fellow scavengers, I told them he was dead and believed it... but I was wrong. He returned that night, looking a lot like you do now, and tore through the crypt, slaying one kid after the other. Bullets couldn't stop him, knives couldn't stop him, fists couldn't stop him... In the fray, while all around me were dying, I grabbed a broken piece of wood... and drove it through his heart. And believe it or not... that killed him." He went into his pocket and produced the broken spoon. "This is your only way out, padre," he said. "It's yours if you want it."

Cisero stared at the thin, jagged piece of wood, then turned his glowering eyes back to Frank, dropping his jaw and letting out a wail of pure hatred. Dropping his shoulders and throwing up his claws he charged, rushing the King of Broken Glass with every intention of pounding him into a fine dust.

Before he'd taken two steps, Frank flicked open the collar of his shirt, revealing the silver cross around his neck.

The sight hit Cisero like a shotgun blast to the face. He halted, tipped and fell to the floor, throwing his claws up over his eyes and scrambling back into the corner, where he cowered, whimpering in fear and pain.

Frank laughed, tilting the cross towards his own face. "Hurts, doesn't it?" he said. "You should have held onto yours." He took a step towards the simpering wreck on the floor. "I don't think it's got anything to do with God. It's the silver. Your kind just can't stand it."

In saying it, his mind's eye brought up the memory of the silver pocket watch Kolbi had discovered before the shark attacked. The pocket watch Frank had been wearing that night when Kolbi returned and killed everyone but him. Because he couldn't stand the silver.

"Weird, huh? If you'd been a bit more generous with your boys and bought them real silver crosses instead of tin, they'd probably still be alive." He smiled. "Which, when you think about it... kind of lets me off the hook, huh?"

Cisero said nothing of any merit. The only sounds to escape his slime-smeared lips were helpless moans.

Frank sighed. "This is a mean world, padre, and full of monsters. Welcome to the club of most of us."

He dropped the broken spoon on his way out, thinking the priest might yet find some use for it. He left the door open behind him.

He followed the trail of dead altar boys through the bowels of the chapel and up into the nave, where the Savior on the Cross regarded the carnage with sad, vacant eyes. Frank, feeling better than he'd felt in a long while, blew the old guy a kiss before stepping out into the night.

Gods of the Damned

"In the earth she softly slumbers,

To the earth we shall return..."

Regan woke to the sound of fireworks. His stomach lurched. He rolled onto his side and coughed bile into a copper pot by the bed.

"You want breakfast?" Deek called from the next room.

"Yeah," he called back, between saliva-slick sputters. Rubbing a hand across his aching iron belly, he sat up and drew the blinds from the window.

In the street below, people were dancing towards the square, waving magnesium sparklers and chanting songs of Old Town. The smoke from a thousand ceremonial bonfires rose from between the buildings. If he looked across the rooftops, Regan could make out the imposing shape of the Norrland Dam – a menacing black rectangle beneath a deep red sky. Shrill screams cut the air, announcing the launch of half a dozen rockets. He let the blinds fall before they burst and stalked through to the kitchen.

Deek set a bowl of bread soaked in milk down on the table. "You sure that's all you want?" His voice had a shade of concern to it, though Regan found it difficult to read any expression in his face, which looked like a mess of half-melted razor-blades.

"It's all I can digest these days," he answered, easing himself into the apartment's only chair. His body creaked as he did so, echoing in the barren, rust-colored hovel his companion called home.

Deek staggered back to the counter on his uneven legs. "Have some coffee at least?"

Regan slid his spoon into the bowl of gray slop before him, lifted it up and turned it, letting the sodden lumps drop with queasy little *slaps*.

“It's gonna happen today,” he said.

Deek turned. “Today? You sure?”

“Yeah.” Regan put the spoon down, letting his hand drift absently back to his gut, feeling its distended smoothness. “Soon. This morning, maybe.”

“Is there anything I can do?”

“Only what you've been doing.” He did his best to smile. “It's okay. I'm not afraid.”

“Well anything you need, just say the word. I mean it. You're safe here.”

There was a knock on the door, loud enough to shake the paper-thin walls of the five-story shack in which they and maybe three dozen others were hiding from the world.

“It'll be Luka,” Deek said. “Wants me to join the parade. I'll tell him to go without me.”

“You don't have to do that...”

“No, it's okay, really.” Deek set down his coffee cup and crossed to the door. “I've always hated festivals anyway.”

He slid open the hatch on the door and came face-to-muzzle with the barrel of a .38 revolver. It barked and sent Deek spiraling across the room, colliding with the kitchen counter and sliding to the floor, his shattered head spurting dark liquid.

Regan looked at his friend's twitching body, looked at the door... and decided not to get up.

With a crash of splintering wood and nails, the room was suddenly filled with shotgun-wielding men in ugly brown suits and ill-fitting fedoras. Cops. The last through the doorway was tall and fat, with a round stone head and a long, tan raincoat. Metal pipes poking out from back blasted clouds of steam into the atmosphere. The pistol in his hand, swinging casually at his side, was smoking. When he saw Regan he grinned, showing a mouth of uneven brown teeth.

“Well, well, well. If it isn't Jed Regan. Imagine finding you here.”

Regan eyed the other man wearily. “And you are?”

The killer in the raincoat gasped, theatrically. “You sayin' you don't remember me?” He flashed a badge. “Captain Elmo Pazzano, Grudgehaven Police Department. We've met before. But maybe you was too concussed to remember.”

Thinking about it, Regan did recall seeing the man on another occasion, from the other side of a picket line.

“What can I do for you, Captain Pazzano?”

The Captain nudged one of the other suits in the ribs. “Like he don't know. Boyfriend ain't but a smokin' stain on the linoleum and he's sittin' here cool as a cucumber.” He holstered his pistol, produced a fat cigar from his inside pocket and pointed it at him. “You got unfinished business in the Grudge, Regan. Certain assurances were given to certain people. The kind of people who won't be put off just 'cause you try to high-tail it to Old Town.”

Regan nodded. “So you're working for the King of Eyes.”

“I'm here in my official capacity. An important union official has disappeared in the middle of an industrial dispute so big it could bring the city to its knees. We've got to get you back to the ID. You've got to take charge of the situation before your boys start a riot that gets half of 'em killed. My interest – and the interest of these good fellahs here – is in keeping the peace. And sure, maybe Eyes kicked in a little somethin' to sweeten the deal. But 'working' for him? That's a stretch.” He flicked open a lighter and held it to the cigar, puffing till the end glowed.

“I'm not going back,” Regan said.

Pazzano laughed. “You don't have a choice. It astounds me that you thought you ever did. The ChaBro bosses told you to sign the deal. Fox told you to sign, your lawyers told you to sign, your friends, plenty of dusties... Even your pal the Mayor told you to sign the deal...”

“Eddie Coll's a stooge,” Regan spat. “I always knew he was. He's the most perfect politician I ever saw, how could he not be? I won't doom my men and their families to lives of slavery under the King of Eyes. He's not going to get what he wants. Not this time.”

“Eyes always gets what he wants,” Pazzano said, staring at the end of his cigar. “That's how come he's King.”

Regan looked around him, casting a glance to each of the suited enforcers, then back to the Captain.

“This won't go how you think. My advice to you and your men is to leave now. While you still can.”

Pazzano leaned against the kitchen table and blew smoke in the old man's face. This close, Regan could hear the pistons pumping in the cop's barrel chest.

“This ain't a negotiation, bub. Them days is over.”

The Captain snapped his fingers and two of his men grabbed Regan under the arms, hauling him out of his chair. The sudden movement sent a stab of pain through his gut. He cringed and almost toppled, but they held him upright.

“Careful with the merchandise boys,” Pazzano said as he moved to the window. “Can't you see he's sick as a dog?” Peering out through the holes in the drapes he saw the three reinforced Roadmasters in the street, each one guarded by another of his men. Crowds of lopsided revelers moved past them, loaded down with baskets and parcels, occasionally pausing to offer greetings or jeers. “What's going on down there?”

“Walk of the Widow's Burden,” Regan answered through teeth gritted against the pain in his abdomen. “Today's the festival for the Widow.”

Pazzano smiled disdainfully. “Old Town crazies and their Old Town gods. You ever hear of the Widow's Burden, Ebnick?”

“No sir,” said the man gripping Regan under his left arm.

“Me neither,” said Pazzano. “But it looks like we picked a hell of a day for this. Take him down to the car.”

While they shuffled out through the doorway, mindful not to trip over Deek's cooling corpse, the Captain stayed at the window, staring up at the sky. It was the color of molten metal, almost like it was on fire. He'd never seen a sky like it in his life.

***

The rust and filth-smeared assemblages that rattled as they passed awkwardly by wore knitted cloaks of black and silver. Their cracked faces were dusted with chalk; exhausts smeared with lavender oil. The traditions of the Widow's Burden – a once-in-several-lifetimes event – dictated the costumes, songs and vocal outpourings of brotherly love (that rarest of all commodities in the Grudge).

However, when Pazzano's men brought Regan out through the tenement entrance, the songs quieted and the outpourings ceased.

“Start 'er up,” Pazzano called to the driver of the first car, feeling the eyes of the Damned upon him. “C'mon, let's go!”

As his men piled into their vehicles, Pazzano was met by a wizened geezer who looked like he'd crawled out of a scrapheap.

“What are you doing?” shouted the old man. Yellow fumes leaked out each time he dropped his jaw. “Where are you taking this man?”

With Regan securely sandwiched between two blockheads in the back seat of the middle car, Pazzano moved around to the passenger side. “Not your concern, old man. Police business.”

“You have no authority here,” the man barked. “He's under the Widow's protection.”

“If the bitch wants to, she can take it up with me directly at headquarters.” Pazzano slammed the door behind him and reached across the driver to honk the horn. “C'mon! Move it!”

Regan stared out at the crowd around the convoy. They'd almost all quit their marching now, and stood still, lined up along the thoroughfare. He observed the swift, yet subtle transformation that reshaped their faces and altered their posture. In a flash, what had looked like a gaggle of passive observers took on the form of a prone mob, readying for the attack.

“You shouldn't say things like that, Captain,” he warned. “The Gods of Old Town aren't like your God. They're real, they're mean and they're powerful.”

“So am I,” Pazzano replied, twisting in his seat so they could face each other. “And I'm the one who'll break your jaw if you can't keep it shut.”

Up ahead, as the driver of the lead car started up the engine, a young boy with a wide, domed head ran out from the sidelines and leaped up onto the hood. One of the passengers, a cop Regan had heard called Osmium, stepped out, drawing his pistol and raising it above his head as a warning. In reply, the kid put a hand under his own jaw, peeled his head back and vomited fire. Osmium, engulfed in flame, fell screaming to the ground as the assembled masses threw themselves on the vehicle.

“Go! Go!” Pazzano yelled as his driver, Hook, put their car in reverse and slammed his foot on the accelerator, sending the Roadmaster hurtling into the car behind. The rear vehicle was shunted back, leaping up onto the sidewalk and crushing three onlookers, as Regan's car swung about and took off down the alley. A black-clad body fell onto their vehicle, splaying its limbs across the windshield and blocking the view of the road. “Son of a bitch!” Pazzano yelled.

Regan turned his head to see the first car, a ruined hulk of flame and black smoke. Some of the Captain's men still moved within its burning skeleton.

Pazzano's pistol roared and suddenly the car was filled with shattered glass. Regan turned back around to see the man atop the hood reaching in through the broken windshield. He recognized him as the fume-vomiting geezer from a few moments earlier. A second blast from Pazzano's weapon tore a hole in his throat and sent him rolling off the hood and into the gutter.

The car skidded, colliding side-on with a grand, sculpted arachnid – part of the parade – then accelerated, smashing through a bonfire and leaving the thoroughfare for a wide alleyway between the buildings.

“The hell just happened?” cried Tucker, the man on Regan's right.

The bar bounced across potholes, weaving between howling, black-clad ghouls.

“We got ambushed,” Pazzano answered. He had his pistol out, breaking the chamber to replace the spent rounds. “Friends of yours, Regan?”

“Servants of the Widow,” Regan said. “She moves through them.”

“Bullshit!” Pazzano called back. “Anyone see Rothschild?”

“Yeah,” Ebnick answered, peering out of the rear windshield as the broken headlights of the remaining Roadmaster, struggling to catch up, came into view. “Yeah, they're behind us.”

They were heading the wrong way – south rather than north – down a street that seemed to get narrower every ten yards.

“Where do I go?” Hook yelled, feeling the walls closing in.

“We need to turn around,” Pazzano said. “Go left. There!” He pointed to a crooked archway up ahead.

The driver slammed on the brakes and pulled hard on the wheel, the car squealing as it turned reluctantly into the tunnel. Rothschild's car followed behind, its rear-end hammering against the bricks as it fish-tailed out of the bend.

The tunnel twisted, sloping down into a redbrick passageway corrupted by dark vegetation, branching off into other, smaller tunnels, too tight to fit a Roadmaster down.

“Dead end,” said Hook.

“No,” said Pazzano. “It can't be.”

“It's a dead end,” Hook repeated, hitting the brakes as a solid brick wall appeared in the beam of their lights.

“Damn it!” Pazzano punched the dash.

“Okay, genius.” Regan allowed himself a grin. “What's your next bright idea?”

“Cram it, Regan.” The Captain wiped the back of his hand across his polished stone brow. “There's nothing for it. We have to go –”

BWWWWOOOOM!!!

The whole car shook, quaking in the reverberations of a cacophonous blast, echoing down the tunnel. All heads turned to see Rothschild's vehicle, speeding round the curve towards them, chased by a rushing torrent of crumbling brick and mortar.

“The tunnel's collapsing!” Pazzano spat the words like they were expletives. “Get out! Go!”

The five scrambled out of the Roadmaster, stealing glances over their shoulders as Rothschild's car was consumed and vaporized by the tumult, headlights snuffed out like crushed fireflies. They raced into a small passageway, dug out of the wall, Pazzano leading the way. He only just managed to squeeze his ungainly bulk through as the ceiling came down behind them, blasting clouds of dust and smoke into their faces and plunging them into darkness.

***

Regan heard the *snick* of a cigarette lighter somewhere among all the coughing and retching. *Snick-snick* and the small flash of blue sparks, but no flame.

“Ebnick? Ebnick, you okay?” Pazzano's voice. *Snick-snick.*

“Yeah, I'm here,” he gasped.

“Hook?”

“Yeah.”

“Tucker?” *Snick. Snick-snick.* “Tucker?” *Snick.* At last the flame caught and Regan saw it in Pazzano's hand as he bent towards the pile of broken rubble that only partly concealed his man's crushed and lifeless body. “Tucker's dead.”

“Why...” Epnick wheezed, choking on dust. “Why did everything cave in?”

“Maybe we should ask our friend here,” Pazzano said, waving his hand towards Regan, sitting awkwardly with his back to the wall. “Any ideas, chief?”

“This is the Widow's land,” Regan said. “Her people, her buildings. She can destroy it all if she so chooses, and *will*... to protect what's important to her.”

Pazzano gave the impression of the attentive, interested listener, nodding as he considered all that Regan had said, then swung out his arm and smacked him across the side of the head. Regan didn't quite see stars, but his vision wobbled as the pain danced within his skull, signaling other pains in his body to fuss and fidget.

“I've had just about enough of this mystical hogwash,” Pazzano said. “Apart from anything else, you ain't even *from* the Old Town! So what in the hell were you doin' here, huh? You raising an army? That it? Gonna march on Midtown?”

Regan smiled in spite of the pain it caused. “Something like that.”

Pazzano snorted. “I knew you had to be stupid to want to go up against Eyes. Didn't realize you were stone cold crazy too.”

Regan laughed. Laughed and laughed. He couldn't help it.

***

The catacombs ran deep and long, snaking their way beneath the town like barren veins in the hide of a desiccated corpse. Once the conduits of a subterranean citizenship, they predated even Old Town and had long-ago been abandoned. Though some sections had been converted by the current population for pedestrian transportation, sewers or landfill, most of the many miles of tunnel were deserted and led nowhere.

Pazzano and his men, with only their instincts to guide them in search of a way out, quickly found themselves wandering in circles.

"Maybe we ought to stay below ground," Hook suggested. "At least until nightfall? Stay out the way of any more crazies?"

"We need to get topside *now*," said Pazzano. "Work out where the hell we are."

"You'll go where she wants you to go, Captain," said Regan, following behind Hook and ahead of Ebnick. "She's leading you by the nose now."

Pazzano sighed. "You deathbed converts are all the same. My old man was like you. He got aggressive fungus in his valves, rotted him out from the inside, took a long time in killing him. He got religion before he died. Convinced the Savior would carry him into the afterlife. But *you*... You got too much faith even for a dying man."

"You said you didn't know about the Widow's Burden," Regan said. "Shall I explain it to you?"

Pazzano let out a bitter laugh and had to halt his steps to catch his breath. "Sure, Regan. Sure. Give us all something to smile about."

Regan cleared his throat. "Well... it's like this... The Widow sleeps. She sleeps like all the Gods of Old Town sleep, for centuries at a time. Then once, every few lifetimes – *today*, in fact – she awakens. She rises from her slumber just long enough to feed, to breed and to answer a few prayers."

Pazzano gave the man a look like he'd broken out of an asylum. "That so?"

Regan nodded. "Now obviously, her time is short and her powers are finite, so not everyone's prayers can be answered. So her followers make sacrifices in the hope their voices will be heard."

Pazzano stared at him a long time, as a grin spread slowly across his face. “And you... You prayed for an end to the King of Eyes, didn't you?”

“Yes,” Regan answered, almost proudly. “I pledged a sacrifice. I made a deal. The King of Eyes will be destroyed. I'm assured of this.”

Pazzano shook his head, turned and started walking again. “Crazy old bastard.”

“I've heard some stories about the Damned part of town,” Ebnick remarked. “Loopy stuff, real cuckoo. But never anything like that. And I mean I've heard all kinds of crazy shit. Heard of cars that talk, dames with sixteen heads, motels made out of...”

“Hey!” Hook exclaimed and rushed forward. “Hey, c'mere! Look at this!” He led the way into a circular hallway sculpted out of the earth, the walls of which were decorated with carved drawings over round doorways. Hook held his own lighter up to the nearest of the carvings. “These have got to mean something, right? One of these has got to mean, like, 'exit,' right?”

“The mark of the Traveler,” Regan deciphered. “I wouldn't advise going that way.”

Hook held his lighter to the next symbol. “This one?”

“The Thief.”

“This one?”

“That's the Widow.” He winced, putting a hand to the ache in his gut.

Hook leaned in closer to the etching, squinting through the gloom at what looked like the outline of a fat spider.

“I suppose you want us to go that way,” Pazzano sneered.

“Might hurry things up a little,” Regan answered, through gritted teeth. “We're going to end up there anyway. She'll make sure of that.”

“The confidence of the Damned,” the Captain mused. “Me? I'm not so sure.” He pointed to the symbol over his shoulder. “The Crypt.” Seeing the surprise in Regan's face, he shot him a smug little smirk. “I got a little schooling myself.”

“The Crypt?” Ebnick shivered. “I don't like the sound of that.”

“It's where they put their dead,” said Pazzano. “And we'll be able to get out the same way they bring 'em in. So let's go.”

***

An hour later they were ankle-deep in remains.

They'd all seen cemeteries before, from the extravagant mausoleums of Blair Park to the pauper's pit at Viermart, but none of them – not even Regan – had ever seen anything quite like the Old Town Crypt.

While the rigors of polite Grudgehaven society dictated that people reserve a certain respect for the dead – their bodies, at least, if not their memories – the Old Towners entertained no such notions. People were, after all, just parts. The Old Towners only threw out what they couldn't re-use. Anything salvageable was cut away to be sold to healers and put where it was needed most. With such a thriving market, many had taken to scavenging through the Crypt in search of anything they could sell off, stripping the dead down to their bones and tossing only what they couldn't get a good price for.

Pazzano, Ebnick, Hook and Regan had expected to walk into a vault filled with neatly stacked corpses. Instead, they found themselves wading through piles of scraps. Most of it was mercifully beyond identification. However, they were still able to recognize the occasional rotted wooden foot, broken rib cage or gaping tin skull.

“This is repulsive,” Pazzano muttered, shuffling his way through the dead. He rounded a stone pillar and pointed his finger at a shaft of red light, filtering down from the far end of the chamber. “There.”

They plowed onward, hearing the sound of parade drums and the chatter of crowds growing louder as they approached the light. It shone through a barred metal door, built into the sloped roof. The remains of the dead, tossed carelessly down the hatch by those with better things to be doing, were piled high against the wall, forming a hill of shredded corpses they'd each have to climb to freedom.

“You first, Hook,” said Pazzano.

“Wonderful,” Hook moaned, and started to climb.

“Then you.” Pazzano pointed at Ebnick, then turned to Regan. “And then you.”

Regan was swaying slowly from side to side, his eyelids drooping, mouth hanging slackly open. “I can't. I mean... I don't think I can.”

Pazzano took a step closer, glowering beneath the rim of the battered fedora that inexplicably had remained on his head throughout the ordeal. “Y'know Regan, I've said it before, but never meant it quite so much as I do now... You look like shit.”

Regan swallowed and moved his lips, but was unable to formulate a reply.

Pazzano gripped him by the shoulders and gave him a light slap on the face. “I didn't come all this way and lose seven good men just so you could lie down and die with the rest of these fossils. Once we've got you back to the Grudge, once you've signed your name to the deal and told all your ChaBro punks to do the same, once I'm *paid* for the nightmare I've endured... then you can die. And I hope it hurts you.”

“How many times...?” Regan murmured, weak with the pain. “We're not going back. She won't allow it.”

Pazzano slapped him again. Hard, this time. “Snap out of it already! The Widow ain't real! None of 'em are! It's a lousy superstition! And even if she were, why would she go to the trouble? Listen to 'em out there! What makes your prayers so much more important than everyone else's? Why in Hell would she give a shit about you?”

Regan grinned, suddenly. His eyes popped wide, glass pupils ringed with madness. “Because,” he said, “I'm carrying her children.”

Pazzano let him go, shaking him loose like he'd delivered an electric shock, then took two steps back and stuck a finger in his face. "It's in your brain," he told him. "Whatever disease you've got. Whatever sickness it is that's eating you alive, it's got your mind now. I'd be doing you a favor if I put a bullet in your skull."

Regan said nothing in reply, but the grin stayed plastered to his mug.

"Captain!" Hook called. Pazzano turned to see the younger man at the top of the hill of body parts, clinging onto the bars of the door. "It's padlocked!"

"Can you jimmy it?"

"Maybe." He let go of the bars, dropping down onto the mound. "I think I just got to..." He was halfway through his sentence when a three-fingered hand shot out from the scrapheap and clamped around his throat. The fingers squeezed, crunching through the thin plating to the thick plastic tubing beneath and tearing it out, spraying thick jets of octane across the earthen wall. Hook's own hands flapped uselessly at his gushing neck as he tumbled backwards down the hill.

Pazzano and Ebnick rushed forward, screaming his name, but froze as they saw the grasping hand rise out from the pile, revealing an arm, shoulder and most of the top of a vulcanized torso, topped by an eyeless head. The half-corpse pulled itself forward with its one arm, scuttling blindly towards them.

Ebnick drew his pistol and fired. The bullet punched a hole in its forehead, but didn't slow it down. Pazzano grabbed Ebnick by the arm, pulling him back as he saw more of the dead lurching out of the shadows, walking with whatever remained of their legs, grasping at the air if they were still lucky enough to have hands and gnashing shattered teeth in anticipation of a kill.

"What is this?" Pazzano was moving back, drawing his own pistol and waving it in front of him. "What the hell is *this?*"

"Servants of the Widow..." Regan's voice was weak. "She moves through them."

“Regan, you son of a...” Pazzano spun about as he cocked the pistol, ready to finally put an end to his prisoner's insane ramblings... and saw no one. “Regan?”

Ebnick fired a second time, doing nothing to slow the approaching horde. “Run!”

“Where's Regan?”

The gun sounded again, flooding the chamber with noise. “Run!” Ebnick crashed into him, shoving him back as the creatures advanced. They retreated back into the catacombs, kicking away pieces of broken bodies quivering with supernatural life.

“Regan!” Pazzano was blind, feeling his way through the shadows, one hand slapping the wall, his other on his pistol and too afraid to search for his lighter. “Damn you, Regan, answer me!”

Behind him, Ebnick turned back, blocking the tunnel and firing three shots in quick succession. Pazzano spun about as he fired his last bullet, seeing the crowd of undead lit for a moment in the blue muzzle flash, before they descended. In the next moment, all returned to darkness.

Ebnick screamed, while his attackers remained silent as they fell upon him and tore his body apart.

The echoes of the carnage were all that chased Pazzano as he ran, propelling himself deeper and deeper into the maze.

***

He wandered for hours in darkness and silence, feeling like a man who'd fallen through a wound in the world. He kept moving, arguing against hysteria that the tunnels ran only so far and so deep. Practicality was a strong barrier against fear.

His lighter, when at last he felt safe enough to use it, burned out after thirty minutes. He pressed on, feeling his way through the black, eyes wide, searching for the slightest hint of light, knowing it would be his salvation.

In the end, it wasn't light that led him out. It was sound.

So soft at first he thought it was his imagination, he soon realized he didn't know the song. Its somber dirge drifted towards him through the darkness and he chased after it like a dog following the scent of meat.

The closer he got, the clearer the song became, till he was able to gauge the size of the choir and decipher lyrics.

“In the earth she softly slumbers,

To the earth we shall return...”

His hand closed on the edge of the wall, indicating a sudden turn. He went around the corner and saw light, soft and red, coloring the surface of the tunnel. He pressed on, the light growing brighter as the song grew louder.

“Servants walk the Widow's Burden,

When the skies and cities burn...”

Pazzano went through an archway and emerged into a wide, round room, with a deep well in the floor and a large round hole cut into the ceiling. He could see the sky through it. Regan was kneeling at the lip of the well and a crowd was gathered up above, around the hole. They were singing as they threw down offerings of food, silk and trinkets. If they saw Pazzano as he approached they clearly didn't care.

He had his pistol cocked and raised in his fist as he closed on Regan from behind.

“Turn around,” he said.

The kneeling man heard him. He raised his head, but said nothing. Slowly, he shuffled about till he was facing the Captain. His shirt was unbuttoned and hanging open. Pazzano could see his bulging iron belly and the seeping lesions that covered it.

“What the hell is wrong with you?”

“I think... I'm in labor,” Regan said. “What... can I do... for you... Captain Pazzano?” Talking caused him pain. He had to take gasps of breath between the words.

“Tell me how I get out of here.”

Regan shook his head. “You can't... Not if... she doesn't want you to... And she wants... you here... Like I said.”

“What do you mean?” Pazzano took a step closer, shouting to make himself heard over the choir. “Where is this?”

Regan grinned. “The Lair... of the Widow.” He hooked a thumb over his shoulder, towards the well. “She's down there.”

Suppressing the urge to pull the trigger, Pazzano kept the gun trained on Regan's head as he walked around him, stepped up to the edge of the well and peered in. He saw a circular stone shaft, filled with cobwebs and clouds of vapor, disappearing down into darkness. Turning back to Regan, he said: “There's nothing there. She's not real. She can't save you.”

Regan laughed, softly, sadly. “I never asked her... to save me... I asked her... to save the Grudge... from *him*... and his kind.”

The choir's song had ended. Now they were watching the two men, enjoying the spectacle.

“A year ago,” Regan continued. “In this very spot... I pledged my life... my *body*... to her. I pledged to sacrifice myself... for her help.”

“All that for the King of Eyes?”

“Not just him... His people... Those who envy him... Those who profit by him... Those *like* him... People like *you*...”

“You really that crazy?” Pazzano scoffed. “You're talkin' about more than half the city.”

Regan nodded. “The Grudge will *burn*... and be made pure by the fire.” He jerked at the pain in his gut, spat froth from his lips and raised himself up. "I wasn't running when I came back here... I was fulfilling... my end of the deal."

"You won't get the chance," Pazzano said, and pulled the trigger.

Regan lurched back, sparks flying from his temples as the bullet hit, ripping the top of his head away. Metal shavings tumbled upward into the air as thin green jelly poured in rivulets down his face. Shoulders slumping, jaw gone slack, he wilted onto his back and lay there, as the last breath ebbed from his throat.

Fearing an attack from behind, Pazzano spun around, pointing his gun at the Widow's followers gathered above. None of them moved or spoke. Not a one seemed the least bit troubled by his actions.

Lowering his pistol and producing his badge he cried: "My name is Captain Elmo Pazzano of the Grudgehaven Police Department! I am here conducting official police business and I am willing to pay a hundred dollars to anyone who can get me out of here!"

The cloaked and powdered crowd regarded him without emotion. After a few seconds, they turned, acting as one, and began to walk away.

"Hey!" he called. "Hey, wait!"

They began to sing. A musical accompaniment to their departure.

"In the earth she softly slumbers,

To the earth we shall return,

Servants walk the Widow's Burden,

When the skies and cities burn..."

Pazzano stepped to the lip of the well, his feet balanced on the edge as he called up. "Wait! Damn you all, wait!"

A long, low boom erupted from deep in the well, shaking the ground beneath him. He stumbled backwards, kicking desperately to avoid falling in.

Spinning about, he saw Regan's body – dead, but not quite lifeless. A crack had appeared in his torso, running from his neck to his dick. As Pazzano watched, astonished, the crack widened, his cold belly splitting open and unleashing a black, pulsating mass that seemed to inflate, swelling up and bursting out of him.

Pazzano, battling to keep his balance as the room around him continued to rock, saw the black mass explode into a hundred thousand moving parts. These too began to move, crawling over and under each other, onto their backs and over onto their many legs, then at last organizing into a wave that rushed towards him.

He raised his pistol and fired into them. Again. Again. And again.

His bullets could do nothing against the multitude. The spiders rose up together like a bucking black stallion and crashed down upon him, enveloping him, scuttling up and down his body, flooding into his pipes and wide, screaming mouth.

Thrashing in futile horror against them he staggered back and went over the edge, plummeting down into the well.

Tumbling, spinning, down and down, he fought still, lashing out with his arms and legs, pummeling the air.

Spiders in his clothes, spiders in his throat, spiders in his eyes and under his skin he fell on, down, deeper into the darkness...

...where he *knew* the Widow would be waiting.

All the Wrong Parts

If cab drivers had a Ten Commandments, Number One (in my opinion) ought to be: Thou shalt not fall for thy female fares.

And if there were a commandment I'd break most frequently, that would be it.

I met my wife when she stepped into the back of my cab. Met a hundred or more girls since who offered every kind of temptation. And then... then there was Dolores.

She moved daintily, like a bird, hopping into the back seat with her arm outstretched behind her, shaking the rain from her umbrella out the open door, somehow managing not to get a drop on her clothes. I think they must teach that kind of thing some place.

She was pretty in the way that only comes from money well spent (the kind of beauty you carve with a scalpel and a blowtorch) but pretty too in that youthful way, the way all dames are before all the hope and joy's been beaten out of their eyes.

"Sunquist Building, please," she said.

"Yes, ma'am," I replied, and started the meter running.

We pulled away from the taxicab stand outside the Blanko Dance Hall and started south. She kept her head turned, staring out the window at the rain, while I struggled to keep my eyes off of her. Her skin looked like polished ebony and glittered darkly where light caught the varnish of crushed crystals. She wore a red dress, clinging tightly to her calculated curves, and a white fur coat, complimented by silver and diamond jewelery. Money, money, money.

After we'd passed a few blocks she said: "Some night."

"Oh yeah," I answered. "Sure is." I couldn't think of anything else. All my rehearsed small talk deserted me in her presence.

Before I had the chance to get too upset with myself she asked: "Working late?"

"About another hour," I said. "Going home?"

"Yeah." She sounded miserable. "I wasn't planning to, but they canceled my set. Not enough of a crowd, they said."

"You're a singer?"

"Not for much longer, the way things are going. It's only my second week in the gig and they've had to send me home three times." She sighed. "I had to work so damn hard for this."

"No, no," I said. "It's bad timing, that's all. The strikes, the riots, that business up at the Creeping Vine? People just aren't going out as much with all that shit going on. Don't beat yourself up. I'm sure you're a terrific singer."

She gave a sad little laugh and bowed her head. "Thanks."

"No, I mean it," I insisted. "I bet you're a real knock-out. C'mon, sing me something."

"What?"

"Yeah, c'mon! I'll start you off." I cleared my throat then gave it my best shot. "Hey bartender, c'mon, set me up!" Slapping my hand against the side of the steering wheel. "Pour hydrochloric acid in my cup! Grab a something and a da bada daa... I forget the words. C'mon, you got to know it!"

"I do." She was laughing. "But I'm not singing it."

"Oh, come on! You making me sing on my own?"

"Sorry, no. No way."

"You can sing on stage in front of hundreds of people but you can't sing for me?"

“The people at the Blanko pay,” she said. “You want to hear me you can come catch the show. If I ever get put back on.”

“A schmuck like me would never be allowed in through the front door,” I said.

That surprised her. “You've never been inside?”

“Closest I ever get is my spot in the stand out front.” I said it with a certain amount of put-on self-pity, even though I was actually pretty proud of securing that spot. I'd earned it. “Anyway, I thought the Blanko singers all had chauffeur-driven limos. What are you taking a cab for?”

She shrugged. “I prefer to live dangerously.”

I gave her the most stern, serious kind of look I could manage in the rear-view. “You not been listening to what I've been saying? Things are dangerous enough as it is. You ought to take care.”

Her smile widened. “You sound like my father. You got kids?”

“No ma'am. Never blessed in that department. It's okay though. I barely make enough with this work to keep me and the wife fed and this heap of junk running, anyhow.”

“Oh, you're married?”

I raised my left hand and wiggled my fingers, letting the thin strip of gold-colored metal around my finger catch the light. “Coming up for fourteen years. Sorry to go breaking your heart.”

“Fourteen years,” she echoed, sounding impressed. “Wow. You don't hear about many lasting that long these days.”

“It's a venerable institution,” I said, hoping “venerable” was the right word. “It's done okay by me, anyways. How 'bout you? Got a boyfriend?”

She tensed, the question making her uncomfortable. “Not right now.”

“Not short on male admirers though, am I right?”

She frowned, the edges of her lips threatening to curl into a smile. “You getting fresh with me?”

“Wouldn't dream of it,” I lied.

“There's a speed limit in this part of town, you know.” “Hey, I'm a married man.”

“Yeah, and don't you forget it,” she advised. “What's her name?”

“My wife? Marianne.”

“That's nice. It's a nice name. What's she like?”

“Oh, she's great,” I said. “Yeah, really... Just... she's really good, yeah.” I kept a picture of her in the glove box. I'd shown it to fares in the past, when we'd got talking, when they'd asked. I thought of reaching for it then, but all of a sudden the Sunquist Building was on my right, and then I was pulling in at the side of the road.

“Thanks,” she said, passing a folded bill over my shoulder as she leaped out, umbrella first, onto the pavement.

“Sure. Any time,” I answered, just managing to get all the syllables out before the slamming of the door could cut me off. I looked down at the bill, unfolded it, and realized that I was staring at a hundred dollars.

I hadn't had time to process the information when I was startled by the rap of a knuckle on my window. I turned my head and saw her standing there, waving at me beneath her umbrella. I thought maybe she'd realized her mistake in overpaying me and wanted her cash back. I considered driving away, but reluctantly settled on winding down the window.

“Sorry,” she said, bending down to get a better view of me. “I asked your wife's name but I never asked yours.”

“Uh... It's Louie,” I said.

“Hello Louie.” She held out her hand. “I'm Dolores.”

I shook her hand. Even that slight a touch sent a flutter of excitement through me. “Hi.”

“When's the next night you're not working, Louie?” she asked.

“Uh... Tomorrow.”

She nodded. “Tomorrow's fine. If you're not doing anything, you should come by the Blanko. There's a guy on the door by the name of Breaker. Ask for him, tell him your name, tell him you're there to see me. He'll let you in.”

I gave her a quizzical look, knowing it might turn her off, but unable to help it. “Really?”

“Really.” She grinned. “You can bring the wife. If you want.”

“Thanks. I might do that.”

“Okay. See you tomorrow, maybe.” Her eyes flicked down to the hundred dollars in my hand. “Keep the change.” She straightened up, spun about and strolled off into the rain.

I stared at the bill for a little while longer – just to make absolutely sure – then folded it up and put it in my pocket.

***

It had been a long time since I'd had enough money in my pocket to make a visit to Guv worthwhile but, walking in the front door, it was a comfort to see that nothing had changed. He even had the old election poster on the wall behind the counter. RE-ELECT MAYOR WYNDAM MORROW, it said. YES TO MORROW FOR A BETTER TODAY.

“Isn't it about time you took that damn thing down?” I said.

Guv's head was round and flat, like a big silver dollar, and both his eyes were on the one side. He had to turn his whole body around to see where I was pointing.

“It's an investment,” he said as he turned back. “Every day it appreciates in value. A lot like myself in that respect. What can I do for you, Louie?”

I'd written what I needed on a balled-up piece of paper. I took it from my pocket, unfurled it and read: “A screw-in size 9 copper-plated filter head.”

“Hmm,” he said. “Open or close-ended?”

“Open.”

“Hmm,” he repeated. “Specialist part. Set you back five hundred.”

“And if I haggled?”

“Seeing as it's you? Four nine five.”

I sighed through my nose and produced a stack of ragged bills, with Dolores' crisp hundred on top.

Guv went into one of the many safes behind the counter and came back with a small brown box. “Y'know, if it's a circulation problem, a new filter head's only a short-term solution. Probably rot clean out in a year, then you'll have to buy another. What you might need is a new converter. And *that* I can do a deal on. Say... twenty-seven hundred.”

“Payment by installments?” I said.

He made a face. “You know how I feel about that kind of thing.”

I put the money on the counter. “Then I guess it's just the filter head.”

***

Twelve flights of stairs to reach the apartment. Lowest of the low rent, deep in the Industrial District. Usually that meant putting up with the noise and fumes of the factories during the day. More recently, it meant contending with police sirens, chanted songs of protest and the noise of long, bitter clashes lasting well into the night. We did the same as most of our neighbors – tried to ignore it. I turned three keys in three locks and pushed open the door.

“Hello?” I called. “Marianne?”

The apartment didn't look like much, and it wasn't. Turn left through the door for the kitchen, right for the bathroom or go straight on for the bedroom. The light was on in the bedroom, so I walked in. “Marianne?”

Her eyes were closed. A dog-eared paperback was splayed open on her chest. Less than half of her lay in the bed. Her legs had been bolted into a truss and tilted towards the ceiling. A drip tray positioned under what remained of her ass caught the trickles of corrupted mercury that oozed every so often from the cracks under her thighs. Pieces of her back, stomach and groin – the more aesthetically pleasing, though not essential parts – had been cut away and now littered the room, strewn across sheets stained with oil and anti-freeze, between discarded tools, tattered instruction manuals and more than a hundred screws of varying size and importance. Plastic tubes connected to crudely carved holes in her neck connected to bottles of lubricant and ethanol, strung up over the bed – part of a clockwork mechanism drip-feeding her rusted veins every couple of hours, designed to keep her tired heart pumping in relative comfort.

This was the way I'd left her when I headed out to work in the morning. The way I'd found her every night I'd come home for close to four years.

Every time I saw her I wanted to weep.

Fighting back that impulse, I crossed to the bed, sat down beside her and placed a gentle hand on her shoulder. “Marianne?”

Her eyelids fluttered open. “Hmm? Wha..?” A little rust-flecked drool spilled down her chin. She saw me, blinked, and looked around her. “Oh Louie, oh I'm sorry,” she said, meaning for falling asleep with the light on. Waste of electricity.

“Don't worry about it. It's not important,” I said, and showed her the box. “Look. I picked you up something.”

She frowned, sad and apprehensive. “Oh. Sweetie. You shouldn't have...”

I tore open the lid and picked out the filter head, turning it to catch the light the same way jewelery salesmen did. “This is going to make you feel like a new woman.”

She did her best to smile, making it seem almost painful. “Can we really afford that?”

“Sure we can. Making you better is the only thing we should be spending money on.”

She sighed. “I doubt a little thing like that's gonna solve all my problems.”

“It'll solve a couple of 'em,” I assured her. “Make you more comfortable, get your engine firing on all cylinders again. At least for a little while, till we sort something more permanent. And don't worry about the cost. I got a great deal.”

I reached down the side of the bed and grabbed my toolbox.

She moaned. “You have to do it now? Honey, I'm so tired...”

“No time like the present,” I said, strapping a torch to my forehead and sliding a cupped lid under her arched back. “Trust me. When this is done you're going to feel like a million bucks.”

Too exhausted to protest, she settled down while I got to work, unscrewing the lead plate in her side and exposing an interlocking network of skinny pipes and pistons. Installation instructions were printed on the inside of the filter head's box and I was careful to follow them as I identified and unscrewed the old part. I had to put in a little more effort than should have been necessary working it free, and when it finally slid out of its hole I saw that the open end had been worn down to the nub. I tossed it and pressed down on the nearest valve. Black bile bubbled out of the hole in a long, guzzling stream and poured into the lid. The stink of it – like rotting meat and vinegar – was ferocious, but I held my breath and turned my head to the side, trying not to let my revulsion show. Marianne was deeply embarrassed by the smells of her sickness.

I pressed the valve a few more times to clean out the tubes, scrubbed away the crusted grime around the opening, then inserted the fresh part, gleaming with its factory-fresh newness. It secured into place with a neat little *click.*

That done, I put the lead plate back, slid out the lid (now brimming with bile) and brought my face up to hers to tell her what a great job I'd done. She was asleep. I kissed her forehead, finding it cold and dappled with condensation, then left the room.

I walked through the darkened hallway, turned into the kitchen and switched on the light.

He was sitting at the table.

I froze when I saw him, unable even to process his presence. He looked like every nightmare I ever had, fused together into one long-limbed mannequin and poured into a woolen overcoat. He grinned when he saw me, flashing the kind of jagged-tooth smile that only made him appear more monstrous.

“Hello Louie,” he said.

I answered him with the only reply I could think of in the moment. “Hello Frank.”

“It's been a long time,” he said. “Surprised to see me?”

“A little,” I said. “I'd heard you were dead.”

He raised an eyebrow. “You didn't really believe that, did you?”

“Not really, no.” This was true. Though I'd never had any reason to think the assassination attempt had failed, in my gut I'd always known the King of Broken Glass was still alive. That didn't mean I'd ever expected him to show up in my kitchen. “What are you doing here?”

“Yeah, good,” he said, leaning forward and clasping his hands over the table. “I'd like to get straight to that too. Fact is, I don't really have anyone else to go to. My family, my closest friends and associates... they're mostly dead. The few that are still alive have pledged allegiance to the King of Eyes and are being watched so close that trying to contact them would probably get me killed. I'm out there, working as hard as I ever worked, trying to build back up what was taken from me... and I'm having to do it all on my own. And it's not easy. Worst part is, I got this great idea for a job. Really. The *perfect* job. But I need another guy.”

“That so?”

“Yeah. In fact, I was casing the joint out, thinking about how in the hell I was supposed to work it by myself... when I saw you sitting outside.” He fixed me with a frightening gaze. “In the driving seat of a yellow taxi cab.”

I can't even imagine the kind of look I must have given him. “The Blanko? You want to hit the Blanko Dance Hall and Casino?”

He grinned again. “I saw you and I thought to myself 'I bet Eyes doesn't even know about Louie. I bet he's no idea we were ever pals.' And I guess he wouldn't, because how long ago was it, now? Fifteen, sixteen years?”

“About that.”

“You been straight for almost twice as long as people have been calling him 'The King of Eyes.' Hell, you've been straight longer than I've been getting called 'Broken Glass!'”

I nodded. Truth was, I'd been going straight almost since the moment I met Marianne. In the aftermath of a heist gone wrong I'd stolen a car, not realizing it was a cab. She, not knowing I was a struggling low-level gangster, got in the back and asked to go to 23rd Street.

“I love that story,” Frank said, like he'd known exactly what I was thinking. “I've told it a couple of times. So many couples have such bullshit stories about how they met, but yours? It's a real keeper. How is Marianne?”

A part of me wanted to tell him to go to hell. Part of me wanted to kick him down the stairs. A small part. I glanced over my shoulder, looking towards the bedroom, then crossed to the table and sat down.

“She's not doing so well,” I admitted, confiding in him like he was a friend rather than a murdering psychopath I hadn't seen in almost two decades. “She can't walk, can't leave the house, some nights she's in really terrible pain... and it's getting worse.”

He frowned. It looked almost like genuine concern. “There nothing they can do?”

“It's not any one thing,” I said, feeling the tears welling up behind my eyes. “It's not simple. She... she's just got all the wrong parts. I could fix it, I know I could, but... the *cost*...”

Frank leaned forward. “You need money. You need enough dough to buy her all the parts she needs and the expertise to put her right. I need money to get back in the game, buy guns, men, equipment, and the information I need to destroy Eyes and put myself back where I belong. How is it that we found each other again after all these years just when we needed each other most? And with everything we need – and more – sitting in a vault in the Blanko just waiting for us to take it! You know what that is? That ain't just coincidence. That's the very hand of God at work!”

I cringed. “Gee, Frank, I'm not so sure about that.”

“Only 'cause you don't see how easy it is,” he said, getting excited. “Here, let me pitch to you. Can I pitch?”

I sniffed and shrugged. “Sure, go ahead.”

“All right,” he said, spreading out his fingers to lay metaphorical cards on the table. “The King of Eyes is on the way out. You may not see it yet, but the rot has set and it is deep. This shit with the ChaBro union boys is grinding him down. Everyone's saying he had Jed Regan killed. Worst thing he could have done, 'cause now they'll never back down. And the longer they strike, the more people get hurt, the closer the city edges to a full-scale riot and the weaker he looks. The cops, the papers, the Mayor, everyone who's been on his side, now they're all stepping back. It's not just because of the union, either. Word is his 'personal biographer' – some haughty bitch reporter he's been telling all his secrets to – has 'disappeared.' Meaning... 'Witness Protection.'” He laughed. “The guy was better off before he killed me. Can you believe that? How long have I been dead? Two months? And look at the mess he's made! Empire crashing down around his ears, like the universe itself is working overtime to bring him down!”

“I'm sure you're thrilled, Frank,” I said. “But I don't really know what...”

We waved his hand for me to shut up. “Eyes *owns* the Blanko. It's his premier legitimate enterprise. Millions of dollars are secured and laundered there, on top of all the money that flows in through the booze and the gambling and every other thing he's got going on under that roof. It's not just a casino. It's the King of Eyes' personal bank!”

“Ah.”

“You're damn right!” He snapped. “It's the biggest freakin' bank in town and normally he'd be treating it like one. *Normally* he'd keep a squad of his best, most trusted guys, tooled up with machine-guns in the shadows, watching the action twenty-four seven. Normally, no one would have any kind of shot at making a score. But these ain't normal times. And if his men ain't down here in the ID, trying to keep a lid on things, they're scouring the city for the journo broad or holed up with him in his penthouse, waiting for the D.A. to come break down the door. Or lookin' for me, 'cause even with everything else I'll bet he hasn't forgotten I'm still alive. You want to take a guess at how many goons he's left guarding the Blanko?”

“How many?”

“Two.” Saying it out loud looked like it gave him physical pleasure.

“Get out of town.”

“It's true,” he said. “He's had to pull his most trusted lieutenants out and can't risk replacing them with people untested, 'cause who knows what kind of shit they might pull. I'm not the only guy out there who'd like to bring him down. There's others, guys further down the chain of command might all of a sudden decide they'd like a taste of real power. The Zigguroths, Benny Lomond, Clockwork Joe, any of 'em!”

“Yeah...” I was too dazed to speak. I was thinking of the money, trying to calculate how much the King of Eyes might keep in his vault and unable to come up with any figure that wasn't astronomical. I was picturing it – a stash the size of a mountain, guarded by two exhausted, careless foot-soldiers.

“Right now, there's only a couple people outside his organization knows about this,” Frank said. “It won't be long till everyone finds out. But I haven't told you the best part.”

I felt myself leaning forward in my chair and knew I was hooked. I hadn't agreed to anything, had barely done anything more than listen... but I knew there and then that he had me. “Yeah?”

“I know how to crack the safe.” He spoke the words like they were music.

“Son of a bitch,” I said.

“It's a very simple plan,” he said. “I sneak in, crack the safe, get the money and run out through the front door. You'll be waiting in your cab, sitting in the same spot where you always sit. Nothing suspicious about that. And in seconds we'll be gone. How does that sound?”

“Simple,” I admitted. “But how do you sneak in? How do you get to the safe in the first place?”

He winced and nodded. “Well that's one slight problem, in that I've never been in the Blanko. We might need to bring in a third guy to case the joint from the inside. Someone rich and important enough to make it through the door, but maybe with an ax to grind against Eyes.”

I laughed suddenly and had to quickly stifle it so as not to make too much noise. I held my hand over my mouth and bent forward, shoulders shaking and eyes watering, verging on a fit of hysterical giggles. Frank looked at me like I'd lost my mind, but I could help it. Maybe this was the hand of God at work after all.

“We don't need a third man,” I gasped, when at last I'd recovered my senses. “I'll do it. I can get inside.”

***

The next evening I was standing in line with the rest of them, dressed in my only suit, which I hadn't worn in nearly a decade and was now embarrassingly tight around the midriff. The ambassadors of high society, with their wax-buffed noses turned up and satin-gloved hands twitching, eager to swat me away, were clearly not overjoyed to be in my company.

After a few minutes, word reached the front of the line and a bored-looking bouncer with a spike-studded forehead walked over to ask me what the "big idea" was.

"I'm to ask for Breaker," I said. "Louie's my name."

He stared at me hard for a moment, like he was trying to decide if he ought to just kick me down the street, then turned and went back to the front of the line. A few moments later a second bouncer appeared, equal to the first in terms of size and menacing attributes. They looked like they might have been fashioned from the same mold, except this one had flames on his face instead of spikes. He nodded when he saw me, took me by the arm and led me down the line and in through the doors, ignoring the protests of the primped and pressed behind us.

On the inside, the Blanko wasn't nearly as nice as I'd imagined it. I guess it never could be, but I was surprised by just how closely it resembled every other dance hall in the Grudge. The décor was a little nicer and the food certainly smelled better, but aside from that, the only impressive thing about it was the clientele. I saw movie stars and musicians. There were faces I recognized from the papers – politicians, business leaders, wealthy socialites and mobsters. Caligula Zigguroth sat in a corner booth, two giggling women on each arm.

Breaker led me a table with a good view of the stage, just a few steps up from the dance floor. Both of them were empty.

"You get two drinks on the house," he told me, in a manner utterly devoid of warmth or charm. "Anything else you got to pay for."

I ordered a whiskey sour and glanced at the menu to check how much it might have cost me. There were no prices listed, which was telling in its own way. The waitress who served it looked like she'd strolled out of a dream – blue-tinted skin, long blue hair and a face so flawless you felt the need to turn your head away or forever lose yourself in its study.

I chose to keep my eyes on the stage, beginning to understand why people revered this place the way they did.

Dolores made her entrance after fifteen minutes. The curtain rose on her, in a strapless silver dress, backed by a sympathetic jazz trio. She purred:

“Hey bartender, come on, set me up,

Pour hydrochloric acid in my cup,

The Devil says he's coming round,

Heard a lot about this town,

Looking for a gal who knows how to have fun,

And he read my name on the barrel of a gun,

My soul's just gathering dust in the Lost and Found,

So come on... drag me down.”

She was something, all right. Conversation ceased when she parted her lips. People stopped what they were doing and paid attention. High rollers, when they heard her voice, cashed their chips and came through from the casino. Even the bouncers quit minding the door for twenty minutes to enjoy the show. Seeing her there, I couldn't blame them for abandoning their posts, or for shooting glares of hatred at me when, after five songs, she stepped down off the stage and came to join me at my table. Behind her, the MC said, “Ladies and gentlemen, Miss Dolores Dark,” to extremely enthusiastic applause.

“Are you finished?” I said to her.

She grinned and waved to the blue waitress, who brought her a gin gimlet. “I'll go back on in an hour,” she said. “They break up the set so as not to hurt the action. What did you think?”

“What do I think?” I laughed. “I think you're amazing. Really. Really amazing. I've never seen anything like it.”

She sipped her gimlet. “Well thank you.”

"You're welcome. I mean it. Dolores Dark, huh?"

She rolled her eyes. "Yeah, it's a stage name. My manager picked it. Thought it sounded... I don't know... Mysterious or something."

"It's very memorable," I said. "I like it."

"Thank you. And thank you for coming tonight."

I smiled. "I wouldn't have missed it."

"Good. I wasn't sure. What about your wife?"

"No, she couldn't. She..." I hesitated over whether to tell her. "She can't. She's... not well."

"Oh. Not serious, I hope?"

"Yeah, actually," I sighed. "It is. She can't go out. Can't walk. Can't even leave her bed. And... tell you the honest truth, Dolores, it's getting worse."

Her hand reached for mine. "Louie, I'm so sorry. I didn't know."

I nodded, trying to smile. It was painful to see the pity in her eyes, so I turned away, looking to the dance floor, which was filling up now that the house band was playing.

"She'd have loved this." I could feel myself slipping into melancholy, which came as a surprise. Usually it doesn't hit till I'm on my sixth or seventh drink. "We used to go dancing all the time, back in the day. Not to any place as nice as this, but some real jumping joints. She could do them all, the... jitterbug, the slow drag, the breakaway, the jive... Boy, but you should have seen her."

The clarinetist was playing a slow solo as the couples shuffled back and forth below us, shimmering through the tears in my eyes. I could feel her gaze upon me, but couldn't bare to turn back to her just yet. At last, she stood, walked around the table to me and took my hand in hers.

"Come dance with me," she said.

“What? Oh, no, no, I couldn't.”

She arched an eyebrow. “But I insist.”

“Really,” I said. “I can't. It's been so long. It's been years.”

“Louie, Dolores Dark, the star attraction of the Blanko, is asking you to dance. You can't turn her down, with everyone looking. Her reputation would never recover.”

I cast a glance around the room, seeing all the well-to-do glaring back at us from their tables, awaiting my response. And so I relented.

We went down the steps to the dance floor and joined the crowd. She put her arms around me while I tried to get the measure of the music, counting down the beat and finally putting my foot forward, taking the lead.

“That's it,” Dolores breathed in my ear. “It comes right back to you.”

It really did. For a moment I was transported back in time, back to the good old days. I wasn't holding Dolores. I was holding Marianne. We were young and in love and not afraid to prove it to the world.

I pulled her close, feeling the sting of tears again. “Why? Why are you doing this?”

I felt her shrug. Her body was warm. Her hair had the scent of frosted chocolate. “I don't know. It's nice to be nice, y'know?”

I didn't know. I'd never known anything of the kind.

***

The version of events I gave Frank was carefully edited to remove almost all mention of Dolores. He'd asked me to meet him in a basement bar with some unpronounceable name on the corner of 5th and Gonorrhea. When I walked through the door the cigar-chomping lizard running the joint hooked a thumb towards the back room.

I found Frank there in a gloomy alcove, nursing a large glass of black rum – the kind they use to knock people out for surgery in Old Town. I told him about my evening, giving him the layout of the place, where the exits were, the doors to the backstage dressing rooms, the works. Though Dolores had proven a distraction, I'd still managed to gather a large amount of information, including the positioning of the King of Eyes' men. And when I got self-conscious, thinking I was holding back too much, I told him about Dolores' set.

“Sounds perfect,” he said. “That's the time to do it. When everyone's distracted.”

I laid it out for him, pinpointing the exact moment she appeared on stage and the placement of the muscle. He nodded and took a pen to a napkin.

“Okay,” he said. “This is how we do it.”

I returned home late. Very late. The ChaBro boys were holding a past-midnight rally down the block, but the noise barely registered to me as I trudged up the stairs. I managed to enter the apartment without waking Marianne and stood for a while by the bedroom door, listening to her breathing. The new filter head was doing the trick. She sounded better. But I knew it wouldn't last forever.

As quietly as I could, I went through to the kitchen and took my old Colt .45 out from its hiding place under the ice box. It had been a long, long time since I'd used it, but it looked in good condition. My head a tangle of excited thoughts about Marianne, Dolores, Frank and the money, I cleaned the gun, loaded it with a fresh magazine and went to bed.

***

The next evening I sat in my cab, parked outside the Blanko, hands at ten and two, trying desperately to remain calm. The line at the door was shorter again, a result of escalating hostilities in the ID. I kept glancing at them in my side mirror, hoping nobody picked the wrong moment to try to get a ride home. Trying to distract myself, I turned on the radio and heard Dan Dorian say:

“I'm here with Mayor Eddie Coll, who, as we've just heard, has announced a city-wide state of emergency in response to the ChaBro

riots. Mayor Coll, what would you say to those who've called this an overreaction?"

"*It's not an overreaction, Dan.*" Mayor Coll's voice. "*It's not an overreaction at all. These men have gone far beyond the limits of peaceful protest and descended into bloody-minded anarchy. This can't be overstated. As your own station has reported, in just the last hour they've started burning buildings. You wouldn't call that an emergency?*"

"*With respect, Mr. Mayor, sources within the union have said they are not the ones starting these fires...*"

"*Dan, please...*"

"*They've pointed the finger at agents working for ChaBro, organized crime and even your own administration, trying to turn the tide of public opinion against them.*"

"*Dan, that isn't just cynical, scurrilous and insulting. It's patently absurd! The safety of the citizens of Grudgehaven is my utmost priority. You know even before I took office I was a strong supporter of the ChaBro workers union, but that was before they turned arsonists. I will not waste any more time in fruitless debate while the factories, offices and homes of my people are targeted for destruction.*"

I thought of Marianne, trapped alone in the apartment, unable even to get out of bed by herself. Was I wrong to be panicking? The destruction they'd talked about probably wasn't as bad as they made out and if it was, it was probably happening a dozen blocks away from our building.

I tried to get a grip. *Don't lose it,* I told myself. *She needs you here. You're doing this for her. Remember that. You're here for her sake.*

"Damn it!" I pounded my fist on the wheel and turned the key in the ignition, meaning to abandon Frank and head for home.

I had my foot on the gas when I heard a blast of gunfire and a whole crowd of people scream. I turned to see Frank, charging out through the doors of the Blanko, a bulging black sack slung over his shoulder and a tommy-gun in his hand.

“Let's go!” he cried, limping as quickly as he could towards the car. “Let's go! Let's go!”

I couldn't leave him. I popped the trunk, leaned over the seat and opened the rear right door as I saw Breaker emerge onto the street, raising a shotgun.

“Look out!” I called.

Frank turned as the shotgun roared, spraying the side of the cab with buckshot. Frank answered by hosing the Blanko's entrance with machine-gun fire. Breaker shuddered with the impact of the bullets and went down, along with four others, collapsing in a cloud of blood, ermin and pearls.

Frank was grinning madly as he turned back to the cab, heaved the sack into the trunk and jumped in the back seat. “Go! Go! Go!”

I slammed my foot and swung the wheel, spinning the car around in a wide arc and heading north, towards the hills... and away from Marianne.

***

I saw Frank kiss the silver cross around his neck as we passed under the ornate archway into Blair Park, the Grudge's oldest graveyard.

“Perfectly, since you ask,” he said. “It went perfectly.”

“Five people dead outside the Blanko,” I said, parking the car between a pair of elaborate marble tombs. “You call that perfect?”

“They weren't the only ones.” Frank sniggered. “Relax. It's done now.”

“We need to make this quick,” I said, stepping out. “Buildings are getting torched in the ID. I have to get back.”

“Not a problem.” Frank stretched as he got out the car, then walked a few steps away, taking in the view over the ridge. Blair Park was on the outskirts, high on a hill. From where we were standing, you could see almost the whole city. “Look at that, will you?” He sighed. “I never came up here enough back when I was running things. Should've, but I never did. There's a special feeling you get surveying the land, seeing the

Grudge laid out like she is, knowing it's all for you. A king at nightfall, able to survey his work, see effects of his influence, carving their way across the city."

My eye was drawn to an orange glow in the south east. "My God, look. Frank, look! It's burning..."

"Yep." Frank took a pack of smokes from his pocket. "That's just the start. You can tell he knows. I mean... you can read it in the skyline. When Eyes gets made he burns shit down. That's what he does. And there's not a soul who's seen him as mad as he is right now."

"Frank, I have to get home. I have to get back to Marianne. So come on, just give me my cut."

"No need." He put a cigarette between his lips and lit it. "She's all yours."

"What?"

"Take it. I got what I came for. It's done."

I didn't like the way he said it or the way he was acting. Anxiety twisting into a knotted ball in my gut, I opened the trunk and unzipped the bag.

"Oh no." There was no money. "Frank..." Skin like polished ebony. "Frank, what have you done?" Smell like frosted chocolate.

I drew back in horror and saw Frank's grin. "All the parts you'd ever need," he said. "Trust me. Highest possible quality, better than anything you could get on the open market."

"Son of a bitch. Frank, you rotten son of a bitch!" He shrugged, holding up his hands like he'd been caught eating a piece of pie before dinner.

"Okay, okay, so there's no money. Little white lie. I figured you might be steamed about that. Truth is, I don't know shit about cracking safes. The job was always about killing her."

"Why?" I could hardly speak. The hate, the rage, the confusion... "For God's sake, why?"

He took a long drag on the cigarette. “She's the King of Eyes' daughter.”

“No...”

“I'm afraid so. Princess of Eyes, Dolores Wexford. Daddy's precious little girl. She wanted independence. She wanted a life out from under her father's shadow. She wanted to *sing,* bless her little cotton socks! And he thought he could make it so nobody knew who she really was. But I knew.”

I stepped back towards the trunk, staring down into her open, dead eyes.

“It's not enough for him to fail,” Frank continued. “Not enough for him to lose his empire or even die. He has to suffer.” Another drag. The smoke whirled like a small storm above his head. “Thinks he knows a lot about pain, does the old King of Eyes. Thinks he knows all there is to know about suffering. Maybe this will show him he's got a little left to learn.”

My hands were shaking. “But she was nothing like him.”

“Bullshit!” Frank sneered. “She was exactly like him, right down to the marrow. Don't be fooled by the candy-coated shell. She's the enemy. One way or the other she was always going to end up dead. Least this way, you get something out of it.”

“You didn't tell me,” I said. “Why didn't you tell me?”

He shrugged. “Didn't think you'd go for it. You always were soft in the head for the dames.

Anyways, it's done now. And when you cut her open, I guarantee you'll find more than enough to fix Marianne. She'll be better than before, even. So don't ever say your old pal Frank never came through for you.” He winked.

I cringed.

Frank tossed the cigarette and turned back towards the ridge, taking a deep breath, filling his lungs with the night air.

“You gotta love her, don't you?” he said, meaning the Grudge. “Go ahead and burn, baby!” He called to the skyline. “Burn! You can take it! Burn his sickness out! Burn it all down! You can take it! You'll be back in Pappa's arms real soon!”

My first shot took him in the small of the back, exploding out through his stomach and spraying the nearest headstone with grease and iron ore. He stumbled forward and twisted about, turning towards me as he went down on one knee. His face was a mask of confusion, eyes wide and uncomprehending. He blinked when he saw the Colt .45 in my hand and tried to speak, but when he opened his mouth all that spilled out was bile.

I squeezed the trigger again, putting a hole in his chest. He rocked back, but didn't go down. I fired a third time and a fourth, cursing his name as I watched the wounds erupt in his body. The fifth bullet was the one that did it. His eyes rolling back as his head fell forward, he collapsed, sagging into a broken, bloody mess on the ground.

For the sake of completeness, I put a final slug in the back of his head, then loaded his body into the trunk with Dolores and drove for home.

***

I didn't make it to my apartment building. Police wagons and fire-trucks had barricaded the street, trying to contain the riot that was threatening to engulf the city. When I tried to get through on foot I was blocked by soot-stained giant in the uniform of a firefighter.

“You can't go that way!” he yelled above the sounds of sirens, gunfire and death clogging the air. “The whole block's gone up! Fire's spreading faster than we can respond. We have to pull back. Everyone has to move back!”

I could see it from where we stood – a wall of white flame in the darkness. “My wife was in there!” I cried. “The 13th floor! She was on her own! She can't walk!”

He shook his head, eyes aching with sadness. He knew without even having to check.

“I'm sorry, son. I'm so sorry...”

***

I walked back to the car, shuffling like a zombie through a crowd of running, screaming, desperate people. Loudspeaker voices warned people to return to their homes. Gas grenades told them to run. The cab, weighted with the dead, was where I'd left it. I drove away from the chaos, not giving any thought to where I was going. I let my body take over the decisions, the way it sometimes does when the mind has been numbed with shock.

Somehow I hit the highway and started south, putting the flames in my rear windshield, going past the dam and crossing the bridge that takes you into Old Town. A few miles out it started to rain. I didn't hit the wipers. I kept my eyes straight ahead, staring into a rippling wall of black night, hoping it might wrap me in its arms and crush me.

What's a man supposed to do when he's caused the death of two innocent women? When his whole world's gone up in flames and he's driving into the rain with two dead bodies in the trunk?

You want to die? I said to myself. *Then die. Put your foot down. Spin the wheel. Be a man and end it already.*

I sped up. I dared myself to do it. I wanted to do it. I wanted to die. Finally, I spun the wheel... and turned off, navigating my way through the snaking roads till I found a place to stop.

I cut the engine and bowed my head to the wheel, listening to the drum of the rain of the roof. I couldn't do it. Even with Marianne gone and nothing left to live for, I couldn't find the will to put an end to it. I didn't have the spine for that. All I could do was weep...

***

I jolted awake with the slamming of the door.

“Drive!” she cried. “Go!”

“What?” I looked around, realizing I was still in the cab, the rain still hammering down, no idea how long I'd been asleep.

“Drive already!” She kicked the back of my seat. I looked in the rear-view to see her peering out the window, the hood of a plastic yellow raincoat pulled up over her head. “Get me the hell out of here!”

“Uh, okay,” I said, not knowing what else to say. I started the engine and pulled away from the curb, passing beneath a blue neon sign, advertising some rundown motel.

I drove us back to the highway and started south again.

After two miles she was still tense, staring worriedly out the window.

“We'll uh... be leaving the city limits soon,” I said to her. “You any better idea where you want me to go?”

“Anywhere,” she said. “Anywhere that isn't here. Anywhere that's not the Grudge. Think you can do that?”

The road kept on straight, into the horizon. I checked the fuel gauge and saw the tank was nearly two thirds full. “Yeah,” I said. “I think I can give it a try.”

“Thank you,” she sighed, sinking back into her seat. After another mile she took a pack of cigarettes from her pocket and lit one. “What's your name?”

“Louie,” I told her, watching her in the mirror. “What's yours?”

She pulled back the hood, revealing an abundance of silken brunette curls, green eyes, glistening red lips... and a face of perfect pink skin. “Lena. You can call me Lena.”

She was beautiful...

"Now leaving the Grudge.

Take your sins and secrets with you."

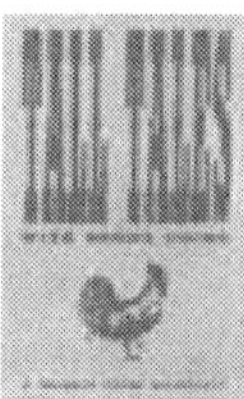

Tall Tales with Short Cocks Vol. 1 ~ Various
Rooster Republic's flagship anthology series. Featuring "Zeitgeist" by Arthur Graham, "The Night of the Walrus" by Gabino Iglesias, and "Mouse Trap" by Wol-vriey. Long live the short cock!

Tall Tales with Short Cocks Vol. 2 ~ Various
Rooster Republic's flagship anthology series. Featuring "The Apple of My iPhone" by Danger Slater, "Laser Tits" by Justin Grimbol, and "The Interstellar Quest for Snack Cakes" by Patrick D'Orazio. Cocks of the world, unite!

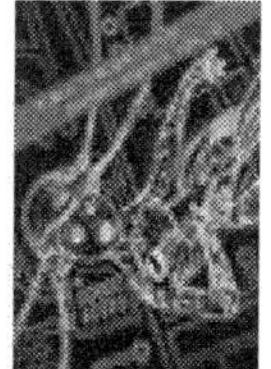

Tall Tales with Short Cocks Vol. 3 ~ Various
Rooster Republic's flagship anthology series. Featuring "The Lycanthropic Air Conditioning Folly" by Jon Konrath, "From God's Ass to Your Mouth" by D.F. Noble, and "Vasectomy" by D. Harlan Wilson. The cock shall rise again!

Clown Tear Junkies ~ Douglas Hackle
Within the whacked-out worlds of these twisted tales, only one thing remains the same: Everything is better when laced with the tears of a clown…

DangerRAMA ~ Danger Slater
KNIGHTS OF THE WHITE CASTLE – An inter-dimensional tale of hamburgers, hubris and science gone mad! SOMNAMBULANT – Terrorists, movie stars, and blue whales converge in this story about a dude who's really just trying to get a good night's sleep. ME & ME & ME & ME & ME & ME & ME & ME – A computer malfunction sends a lone astronaut spiraling across the cosmos. Will he save mankind or just masturbate a lot?

Alice's Adventures in Steamland ~ Wol-vriey
The American Queendoms of New York and Texas square off in this Steampunk Bizarro extravaganza! When war erupts between Victoria Queen of Hearts and Her Majesty Mech-Anna, it sets them down a path of intrigue and violence that threatens to annihilate both dominions. With the help of Lord Busybody and his mechanical assistant Crank, Alice Sin—prostitute/assassin for hire—may be their only hope to fulfill the 'United States' prophecy.

DoG ~ Matt Hlinak
Culann Riordan was a high school English teacher with poor impulse control and a taste for liquor. He fled to Alaska before the state could yank his teaching certificate and toss him in jail. He hires on as a commercial fisherman aboard the Orthrus, a dingy vessel crewed by a colorful assortment of outcasts seeking their fortune beyond the reaches of civilization. As he struggles to learn how to survive the rigors of life at sea and the abuses of the crew, he fishes a mysterious orb out of the depths of the ocean and comes into conflict with the diabolical captain.

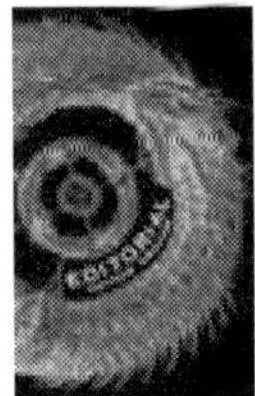

Editorial ~ Arthur Graham
Follow the editor and his client into the infinite ring of Ouroboros, the self-devouring, in this episodic novella by Arthur Graham. A story told through concentric circles of narrative, each one adding a layer of truth while further smothering all notions of certainty, *Editorial* will leave readers wondering just how many times the same tale can be swallowed....

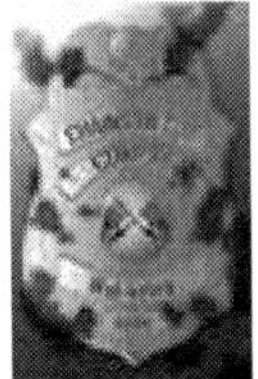

Chainsaw Cop Corpse ~ Wol-vriey
Simon is having a bad fucking week. When you're a D.C. Detective, every week is a bad week, but this week has been a BAD fucking week. For starters, some psychopath has been murdering people, stealing their body parts and smearing their corpses with peanut butter. To make matters worse, the contract killer "Boots" has recently resurfaced, and his girlfriend's chainsaw arm destroyed his bed when he made her climax. And if that weren't bad enough, now he really has to take a shit!

Made in the USA
Lexington, KY
28 February 2014